MISSING IN
PRECINCT PUERTO RICO

MISSING IN PRECINCT PUERTO RICO

BOOK FOUR

STEVEN TORRES

THOMAS DUNNE BOOKS

ST. MARTIN'S MINOTAUR ✺ NEW YORK

This is a work of fiction. All of the characters, organizations, and events portrayed in this novel are either products of the author's imagination or are used fictitiously.

THOMAS DUNNE BOOKS.
An imprint of St. Martin's Press.

www.thomasdunnebooks.com
www.minotaurbooks.com

ISBN-13: 978-0-312-32111-6
ISBN-10: 0-312-32111-2

First Edition: October 2006

10 9 8 7 6 5 4 3 2 1

This book is dedicated to

Damaris,
my love

Diana and Janette,
sisters who shared Puerto Rico with me

and

the too many millions of children who suffer

ACKNOWLEDGMENTS

This book has been made better by the early readers—people who have sloughed through unbound, unedited versions. Some comments were incorporated, some were not. Problems are, of course, all mine, but some of the finer points in the book must be attributed to Buzz DeRusha, Jennifer Jordan, Michele Martinez, SJ Rozan, Sandra Ruttan, Beth Tindall, and Sarah Weinman. My thanks to them all.

The time and confidence to work on this book come from the generosity of my wife, Damaris.

MISSING IN
PRECINCT PUERTO RICO

PROLOGUE

He squeezed into the waiting-area seat across from a family of four. He'd made it with at least twenty minutes before boarding. The magazine in his hands was an old one, but it had good articles about space travel and a splashy cover of a space walk in progress.

The couple across from him were young and their children were quite small. The man supposed they were perhaps four and five years of age for the boy and the girl, respectively. The husband and wife, neatly groomed, svelte, and serious-looking, were still in their twenties. They were having a quiet argument, not drawing attention to themselves, but not paying much attention to the children, either. Not that the children were any trouble. The girl had a Raggedy Ann doll in hand and was able to think up an entire Spanish conversation to have with it. The boy had a Fisher-Price tow truck—low in quality, perhaps, but completely satisfactory to the child.

He pretended to read an article, eyeing the children over the top of the magazine as he flipped pages. He knew precisely how much his sunglasses hid his roving eyes.

At a high point in the argument, about what the man had no idea, the father took his hand out from under the light jacket he had folded on his lap and waved it in the air for emphasis. That moment, the boy launched the tow truck into the air, the curve of his armrest providing a ramp for takeoff. The toy landed at the man's feet, bumping his toe. The man reached the truck before the boy could get out of his seat. He smiled.

"Do you want it?" he asked the boy, holding the toy out to him. The boy took a step with his hand out for it. The man pulled it closer, and the boy took another step.

"¿Lo quieres?" the man asked in accented Spanish. The boy took another step across the aisle. The parents stopped their argument to watch the goings on. The man winked at them. He brought the toy to his lap, and when the boy made a final lunge for it, he grabbed him and sat him on his knee, tickling him.

The parents both moved forward in their chairs, not completely sure what to think of this man who had their son. There could be no danger, of course, this was an airport lounge in broad daylight; a hundred others were waiting for the flight to San Juan. The man ignored their nervousness for a moment. The worst thing he could do would be to acknowledge the hint that there was anything wrong with his actions.

"The most natural thing in the world," he thought to himself.

"He likes his truck," the man said to the parents. His smile was large, showing his teeth. He made sure his wrist was a little limp when he gave the mother a good-natured wave. It paid to be a little on the gay side when dealing with the Latins. They probably figured his love of children, his desire to hold them, tickle them, spend time with them, was a sign of maternal instincts in him.

He handed the truck back and gave the boy a final hug, putting his face next to the boy's, and taking a moment to feel the skin of the boy's forearm as he handed him back to his mother.

"His skin is so soft, so rich in color." He passed his hand over the flesh of his jaw. "I hope a few days in La Isla del Encanto will give me skin like him." He smiled. All of this was said to the mother and with a little bit of a lisp—one woman to another, as it were. The father leaned farther forward and spoke.

"Are you going to be in Puerto Rico long?" he asked. His English was comfortable, but clearly not his first language.

"A few days," the man said.

"Business or pleasure?"

The man smiled. He wondered why everyone broke down their trips into those two confining categories. He told the truth.

"Both," he said. "Both."

SAN JUAN, PUERTO RICO

She came out of the surf and toward him; her five-foot-ten frame, slender and well shaped, held onto pearls of water, slowing their descent along her curves. She was smiling, and why not? She was in love. Love so strong, she told him more than once, that sometimes it hurt. A cliché, perhaps, but they were sharing their honeymoon in paradise. She fell onto the blanket next to him and nuzzled. She picked up a red flower they had found earlier and stroked his face with it. It was his time to feel the hurt of love.

There was a life, currently just beyond his reach, in which he could be happy with her, no fears, just love.

She tied a light wrap around her waist. They picked up the blanket and the empty wine bottle they had sacrificed some hours before and made their way off the sand and onto the sidewalks that led back to the hotel. They drew very few looks in their bathing suits and flip-flop slippers—hotels lined the beach and the sight was common. They claimed their key at the front desk, embraced and kissed in the elevator until they arrived at their floor. In the room, she drew him to the bed to continue the romance of the trip up. They kissed a few minutes more, then she started to untie her top. He stopped her.

"We're salty," he said. It was true, proven by the flavor of their kisses.

They showered together. Sex was good, though he was as distracted as he had been on the beach. She made up for his faults and didn't even notice.

They dressed for dinner—a table reserved at the hotel's restaurant.

"Dancing later?" she asked.

"I'm getting up early tomorrow, remember?"

"Still?" she said. They had never talked about him not rising early, but the disappointment of his not having chosen to stay with her in the morning was evident in her voice.

"Still. I told you. I have to work. Two days out of fourteen and the company picks up the bill for the whole trip. That's not too bad a trade."

"But it's our honeymoon," she complained while putting on an earring.

"But it can't be helped," he said. "And I can't afford not to do this." He told the truth there at least. She nodded her acceptance.

In the morning, he kissed her forehead without her waking and got into his rented Toyota, driving off with just a small bag with a change of clothes. He had taken care to leave his bride with more than enough money for the next two days. From the hotel, everything she could need was within walking distance—not just the beach, but stores and restaurants as well. The only thing that would be missing was himself, and at the moment that he drove away from the hotel parking lot, he didn't think that was so great a loss.

AIBONITO, PUERTO RICO

She knew what was coming. Ana Lopez was twelve, and for the few years she could remember, her parents had thought of her as an extra pair of helping hands. She was just then learning about slavery in the seventh grade, and the class gave voice to her sentiments at the moment when her father called to her.

"Ana," he said, holding out a twenty-dollar bill and a list. "We need milk, bread . . . Here's the list." The list had eight items, including some cans and a ten-pound bag of rice. Too much for her. This only meant she would have to take her brother. She loved her brother but did not love being responsible for him on the walk to the store and back.

"Don't forget to count the change," her father said. What he meant, she knew, was that he would be counting the change when she came back, so there should be no candy bought with the leftover money. Was this not work without reward? Was this not the essence of slavery?

Of all the chores, going to the store at night was not the worst. That didn't make it good. There was a kilometer of roadside walking to navigate in the dark. There was no sidewalk, so you had to keep to the edge. There weren't many cars, but the ones that did pass, did so at speeds that showed more confidence than prudence. Without street lamps, cars were hardly the only danger. What if a pack of stray dogs passed by on their way to some bitch in heat? Worse, what if a bat swooped too low and got caught in your hair? Or a flying roach?

Worse than roaches, bats, dogs, or dark were the men of Colmado El Brinco. The store, like many rural stores on the island, was a little bit of everything. There were two pool tables, a few card tables, a jukebox, and the store's checkout counter had gained a growth of stools in front, doubling as a small bar. There was a row of rums and a bottle of gin behind the counter, and drinks were served in plastic cups, sold by the inch. They could be mixed with water, soda, juice, or an ice cube, but requests for these were rare. Most drinkers thought the drinks were diluted enough, though they could never prove anything, and never mentioned anything to the store owner, who also poured the drinks, unless they were far drunk. The drunkenness was, of course, proof that the drinks could not be that watered down.

The drunks were the worst part of Colmado El Brinco. They were regular men from the barrio, but they leered. It was a look that one of Ana's girlfriends had explained to her a few weeks earlier. Before that, she hadn't had a word for the look, and she didn't know why it disturbed her. Her friend had given her a few phrases to use whenever anyone leered at her, but in the trips to the store since the lessons, Ana hadn't had the presence of mind to do anything but keep her eyes on the counter in front of her and march out of the store, meeting no one's eyes as she left.

As she walked the kilometer with Raulito in tow, she thought of what she would say if any of the leers turned into words or actions.

In a white panel van parked a few yards beyond the store, two men sat, speaking Spanish, one trying to convince the other to go through with a plan they had agreed to put into action. They watched the children approach and go into the store.

"You have to," the driver said to the passenger.

"I'm a patriot," the passenger said. He looked away into the darkness of the roadside woods, then he looked back.

"You have to," the driver said again, each word emphasized. It wasn't a question of patriotism. The passenger understood this, and after a moment, he nodded.

Inside, one of the drinkers at the counter made way for Ana and Raulito.

"*Llegó la doña,*" he said, leering. *The mistress is here.*

Ana kept her eyes on the counter. The man speaking was in his fifties or more.

"*Está ya mujercita,*" he said. *She's already a little woman.* He pursed his lips to point to Ana and then pointed at her chest, where there was nothing yet that she was proud of. She could feel the blood rush to her face, and words began to rise in her. The store owner kept ringing up the groceries.

"*Me gusta,*" the man said. *I like her.* He leered harder than ever.

"*¿Tú no tienes esposa?*" Ana asked. *Don't you have a wife?* She already knew the answer.

"No," the man said.

"*Con razón,*" she said. *With reason.* Several other men in the store laughed at her wit. She knew she had won the match, no matter whatever else the man might think to say. He didn't think of anything. Instead, he tried to finish a drink he had already gotten to the end of. Ana handed one bag with the ten pounds of rice to Raulito, and marched out, head high, chin up, one man actually clapping his approval.

Brother and sister pulled over onto the grass a few minutes later as the headlights of a van illuminated them from behind. The van stopped.

"We'll drive you home," the driver leaned over to say through the passenger side window.

Ana looked, but couldn't see a second person until the side door opened. A younger man was there. It didn't make any difference. She wasn't about to get into a van with men she had never seen before.

"We live near," Ana said and started to move on. The van followed closely a few seconds.

"You don't have to walk," the driver tried again.

She ignored this. The van driver angled the vehicle onto the grass, cutting off the path home.

"Take the boy," he said.

The younger man jumped out the side door and took hold of Raulito. Raulito dropped his bag of rice and was tossed into the back of the van a little harder than either the driver or the younger man wanted. Ana screamed.

"Raul!" She stepped toward the younger man, her groceries still in hand. The younger man backed himself into the van; there was fear in his eyes as though Ana, so small, so frail, could hurt him with the intensity of her look. She would have hurt him, but wasn't given the chance. From behind her, the driver had grabbed her by both upper arms and tossed her into the van. Her groceries dropped to the asphalt, bottles breaking.

The van traveled at a high rate of speed for five minutes, then slowly over rough terrain for an hour. Raulito was easily subdued with one smack and tape over the mouth and binding the hands. All the way, Ana fought. She screamed, so that the tape went over the mouth crookedly. The hands were taped together, and when she used them to sledgehammer the younger man, he wrapped tape around her torso, trapping her arms at her sides, keeping them from moving. She kept kicking throughout the trip, the young man unable to bring her legs together. When the van finally stopped, the side door opened again and Raulito was dragged out headfirst. Ana kicked the younger man in the jaw as he tried to pull her out; he fell back. She bolted out of the van and rammed her head low into the driver's gut. He cursed and clutched her hair as she tried to pass; he slapped her and pushed her to the ground hard. There was blood on her face when she bounced back to her feet. He grabbed for her again, and she kicked him in the groin as her friend at school had taught her. He knocked her to the ground again, and she rose; he knocked her down again, and this third time, when she got up, she bit into his hand, catching his right pinky. Pain shot through his arm like a heart attack, blinding him, making him feel like his life was about to end. He reached for a short knife strapped to his ankle.

It was still work to get her jaws to open, even when he had pulled the knife out of her throat and she had at last stopped moving.

CHAPTER ONE

There was a time, when the Spaniards still ruled Puerto Rico, that the hill town of Angustias had nearly twelve thousand souls counted. This included men, women, children, and eighteen slaves. There were a little more than nine thousand citizens in the Angustias of 1982. The drop-off in population could be traced back to many factors—fewer farms needing fewer workers, the unforgiving mountainous geography, and the lure of far-off places like New York and Miami with promises of better jobs and futures that didn't include the daily wrestling with Mother Nature for the sake of a few dollars on which to live. Also, in the modern age, people simply had fewer children. Contraceptives were available in Angustias, as elsewhere on the island, and most, Catholic or not, used them. Gone were the days of twelve children in a family. Now, even a half-dozen raised eyebrows.

Luis Gonzalo, sheriff of Angustias since 1964 when he took the job at the age of twenty-two, had been part of a small family himself, his father having died young and his mother never remarrying. He had been born and raised in town. He had seen the best and brightest go off to college in some larger town and only ever come back for Christmas, New Year's, and Three Kings' Day. He had sent several of *los Angustiados,* citizens of Angustias, to prison. He had put one in the grave. When the last census announced that the town's population had fallen for the fourth straight decade, Gonzalo thought of the family he had formed in Angustias—two teenaged daughters and a daughter born just the year before. They would get the best educations he could afford for them. Chances were low that they would come back after college. And there was nothing he could say that would change that. Even if there were, he wouldn't say it. Children had to live their lives, and if they thought it would be better to live it elsewhere, he wasn't the one to stop them.

Almost every afternoon for the first few years he was sheriff, Gonzalo toured the stops to watch the children as they climbed onto the school bus in the morning and then as they got on at the school to go home in the afternoon. This was a task he enjoyed, but one he now shared with his two deputies.

On this afternoon, there was only one small problem as the children of the elementary school waited for the bus, and Gonzalo was there to tend to it. Two boys, part of a group playing with marbles, got into an argument. To end the argument, one of the boys, a nine-year-old, picked up an aggie and tossed it into the woods. The aggie owner thought this deserved a punch in the nose and gave it to him. Gonzalo left his conversation with the school principal to break up the scrabble before a crowd had formed. He held each boy by the collar, pulled them apart, but one tried for a final kick, which landed on Gonzalo's shin. Had he not been involved in this disturbance, he would have noticed a dark-skinned man in a big American car, who parked in front of the school for a minute, wrote down a few notes, made a three-point turn, and drove off. Gonzalo didn't see this, nor did the principal. The children who noticed it, said nothing.

So much passes beneath the eyes of the local police. So much that they want to do something about, but can't. When, for instance, a woman of the town, a respected woman with children, begins to go out at night with another man from another town. Or when a man has lost his job and begins to drink more than he can hold. Or when a young girl, falling in love for the first time, falls for the wrong young man. What can the officer do? Even when he has been friends with the man for many years, and has a good relationship with the wife in question, he is powerless to do more than talk to them as a friend and as an acquaintance. Drunkenness is only illegal when it's public, no matter how much damage it may cause in private. As for a woman leaving the house when her husband is away and finding comfort from some other man, there are no laws broken there either, no matter how tragically things may turn if the husband finds out. As for the daughter of the family, the one falling for a boy with a police record that, however slight the offenses, can't just be ignored, there is even less that can be said to her. Even if she is the goddaughter of the sheriff of Angustias, Luis Gonzalo, the boy's records are sealed by the court and an officer can't just blurt out this type of information.

After advice, the best an officer can do is watch the family drama unfold, ready to step in with the force of law at the first sign of trouble.

The family in question, the Cruz family, had come close to requiring Gonzalo's intervention in the past few weeks. There had been arguments that the neighbors had complained about. Gonzalo had gotten there as quickly as he could, but the fights were over each time, Guillermo Cruz sitting in his La-Z-Boy, Amelia washing dishes, before Gonzalo knocked on the door. There had also been a call to the station house to say that Giselle Cruz, the daughter, wasn't home yet though it was nearing eight at night and school had been over for hours. By the time Gonzalo drove to the house to get a more complete report, the girl had arrived and locked herself into her room.

Today was Giselle's *quinceañera*—her fifteenth birthday—a cause for celebration much like the sixteenth birthday is celebrated for young ladies in other countries. Amelia and Guillermo were determined to make the party one that Giselle would remember with fondness for the decades that were to come. Between the drinking, the paramour, and the boyfriend that didn't quite measure up, Gonzalo felt certain the night would be remembered. He wasn't sure about the fondness.

He thought of all of this as he made himself a cup of coffee, straining the grounds through a *colador*. He was dressed in his best civilian clothes and didn't want to spill a drop on himself. He heard Mari coming toward the kitchen in her slippers and started to move faster and think less.

"You're still not done making that coffee?" she asked. "We're going to be late."

"We have half an hour before it starts," Gonzalo answered. "Besides, it's a *quinceañera*. It'll last for five hours or more."

"Yes, and we're the godparents. We have to be there for the whole thing."

Gonzalo rolled his eyes at the thought of trying to find that many hours of interesting conversation at a young girl's party where the attendants were either children or adults trying to duck out as soon as the food and the liquor were gone. And he had seen the amount of liquor Guillermo had packed away into the back of his station wagon a few days earlier. It would last a while.

"You know how this night is going to end, right?" Gonzalo asked his wife as she took a long sip from his cup of coffee. She twitched her nose, a sign that she waited to be enlightened.

"I'm going to be driving people home, if I'm lucky. If I'm not lucky, there'll be a fight or two for me to break up."

"It'll be nice," Mari said. She handed him his cup, half-finished, and left him to drink down the rest.

On the Cruz family's wide front lawn, a white canopy had been set up, musicians were tuning instruments, there was a giant cake on a center table, several long tables held a buffet, another table held the sodas and juices, and another one held the liquors. To the left of the house, there was an entire pig being turned on a spit by a man Gonzalo didn't know. The man's shirt was open, and he had a beer and a knife on a little table standing next to him. The band played the opening notes of a popular salsa song, then stopped. Apparently, this was a sound check. Mari and Gonzalo arrived at the house and found the Cruz family.

Guillermo had a plastic cup with a clear liquid in it. He noticed Gonzalo's look.

"Seven-Up," he said. Gonzalo nodded. It was seven in the evening, and if Guillermo could hold off drinking for a couple of hours, there was a chance the night would pass peacefully.

Soon, more people arrived, arranging themselves at different tables on the lawn, closer to the food or the soda or the liquor or the family, as they desired. The roast pig was carved bit by bit and served to each table on large platters. Amelia's lover stopped by for a minute. Gonzalo noticed that Amelia didn't look his way and instead held tight to her husband's arm. The lover walked back to his car, his look forlorn. Mari reported later that Amelia had told her the dates with that man were at an end.

"That was just the foolishness of a woman who . . ." She never finished the sentence.

Giselle's boyfriend arrived in good time and gave her a chaste kiss on the cheek in front of her parents. Gonzalo was happy to see that the boyfriend was not the young man it had been just a few weeks earlier. Instead, this was a worthy young man, just her age and never in any trouble with the law.

The time came for Guillermo to help Giselle in the ceremony of changing her shoes from those of a girl to those of a woman. Then there were the presents to deliver and the wishes and the toasts and the father's speech and the mother's speech and finally the cake. Throughout the night, Guillermo had nothing stronger than a Pepsi. Later, he explained that he had given up liquor, cold turkey.

"Ten days ago I got drunk and fell into the ditch across the road. I sprained my ankle, skinned my elbow, and I was crying. Giselle came out to help me. My eyes were unfocused, and I had vomited. The lowest part of my life, I think. What am I supposed to do when my own daughter is pulling me out of ditches? I just said, 'No more.'"

"And you haven't had a drink since?" Gonzalo asked.

"Nope." Guillermo walked off to greet a latecomer to the party. Near midnight, two men who had not followed Guillermo's example got into an argument and shoving match over who was the greatest of Puerto Rico's writers—Zeno Gandia or René Marqués. Gonzalo had an opinion on the issue, but he kept it to himself, separating the two men quickly and having them driven home. Minutes later, Guillermo called the party to order, thanked everyone for the gifts and for their presence, and led them in singing "*Feliz Cumpleaños*," and people got the idea that it was late and they should go home.

At the very end of the party, Giselle, her boyfriend trailing close behind, found Gonzalo and thanked him for his gift. It was the best of the whole day, she declared.

"Your parents gave you the party," he reminded her. "And they gave you life."

"Second best, then," she said, and she gave him a kiss on the cheek.

"*Que Dios te cuide*," he said. *May God protect you.*

Mari walked up to him a few minutes later.

"You gave her the booklet?" she asked.

"Yep. Five hundred plus dollars in her own little bank account."

"Did you tell her how you've been saving since the day she was born?"

"You think it would matter to her?"

Mari shook her head, then she dragged her husband to the car so they could go home.

That night, while Gonzalo celebrated the life of his goddaughter, Tomas Villareal and his wife drove away from home. One daughter and her little brother had gone to sleep, and the oldest daughter was in charge of the house. They lived in a remote part of a remote town and little could happen to them. If some accident occurred, the children knew the phone number of the police precinct.

The eldest child, Marisol, had plans for the evening and put them into effect as soon as she was sure her parents were well away. She made a phone call and confirmed a rendezvous.

"I love you," she said with a smooch over the phone. When she hung up, her little brother, Samuel, was right behind her.

"What are you doing out of bed?" she asked. The answer didn't matter. She knew he wouldn't sleep again for hours, and if she didn't think of anything, the rendezvous would have to wait, though every cell in her body told her it would be wrong to wait. A moment's thought gave her a plan, and in another moment she had put it into action. Her brother, at the age of seven always up for an adventure, was up for this. It was only a few minutes later, in the dark of the forests, that he started to rethink the plan.

In the darkness of the woods, he stumbled over a root. He put out his right hand to keep himself from falling and caught it on a thorn on the trunk of an orange tree. He didn't yell out, though the thorn had gone completely through the flesh of the heel of his palm. He was too tired to yell. Instead, he stopped in the woods and brought the hand up to his face for closer inspection. He was desperate to rest, and he was sure he wouldn't be denied if he showed her the blood.

"Keep moving," she said, pushing the back of his head forward. Again, he almost fell.

"But I'm bleeding," he complained.

"Keep moving." Another shove.

"Look at my hand. There's a hole. I'm bleeding."

"I don't care if you're dying. Keep moving," she told him and gave him another shove.

He started to move, still examining his hand in every stray beam of moonlight. After another five minutes of marching through the woods, he stumbled again. When he put his hand out this time, he missed the tree in front of him. Instead, his right arm grazed some bits of bark off the trunk, and a portion of the skin near his elbow was peeled back. He couldn't help crying out in pain and crying generally even though he had been warned to make no noise. He wanted no more than to sit on the ground and examine the wound. He crooked his arm to bring his elbow closer to his mouth. He was missing about two or three square inches of skin, and the spot burned. He wanted to blow on the wound.

"Get up," she told him.

"I'm hurt," he said.

"Don't care. Move." He could tell anger was rising in her.

"I think I got a splinter. It hurts."

She tried to grab him by his hair, but his mother had recently given him the only haircut she knew how to give, a short crewcut. He had on no shirt, only a pair of blue shorts that reached to his knees, and his sandals. She jerked him up off the ground by his bony, little boy's arm and pushed him farther on into the woods.

"I want to go home," he complained.

"No."

"I need to rest."

"No."

"Just a few minutes."

"No."

"Please."

"Look. We're almost there. Once we're there, you can go to sleep, okay?"

"I don't want to go anymore."

"Too late. I'm not taking you home until tomorrow. I told you already. Stop whining. Be a man."

He thought about the last command: "Be a man." How do you refuse to follow that kind of order?

He walked on in silence a while longer, his punctured left hand holding his scraped right elbow. Certainly he wanted to be a man, but he was tired, thirsty, and in pain. Both his ankles had been twisted more times than he could remember in this trip into the woods. He was sorry he had agreed to come out this far. He turned 180 degrees and started walking back the way he came. He ran into her in the first step and tried to get around. She grabbed him by both elbows and shook him.

"Be a man," she said through gritted teeth. "Be a man, or I'll hurt you."

He started to cry in earnest, more from frustration and tiredness than any of his physical pains.

"I can't be a man."

"Try."

"I'm only seven," he blurted, ashamed.

"But you'll be eight in a few weeks. Look. The shack is only a few minutes away. It's much closer to go there than to go home. Then you can sleep all you want, okay?"

She pushed him again, deeper into the woods, uphill now. In a few more steps they came to a fence. Three strands of rusted barb-wire, strung along thin, rough-hewn sticks standing amidst tall grass. She held up the top wire.

"Go through," she whispered hoarsely.

He bent down low to perform a move he had done a thousand times before. This field, the shack in it, were secret hiding places for him. He stepped one foot through the gap in the fence and tried to swoop the rest of his body through, but he went an inch too low and scratched his forehead. His reaction to jerk away from the wire, up toward the one being held for him, made him catch his shoulder on the wire. His reaction to that pain was to throw himself through the fencing to the other side. This gave him a long scratch down his trail leg. He wanted to lie in the grass and examine his wounds, but two hands dug themselves into his armpits, lifting him off the ground and pushing him forward.

There was a gentle slope up to a concrete house with a shiny corrugated zinc roof. Between the fencing and the house, there was a shack that seemed decades old but had, in fact, been made recently out of the best pieces of wood from a house demolished a few months before. The paint was chipped and faded, but the structure was sound and the zinc roof was shiny and new, with the smallest of inclines to run the rain off.

The shack sat in a clearing under the bright moonlight, and the boy reached it first and pulled back the simple bolt lock. He swung open the door he had swung open many times before and peered into the darkness of a room he had hidden in for hours on end. He could just make out the hammock piled in a corner, a fresh bunch of bananas hanging from a rafter, and some sacks of musty, picked coffee lined up against the wall. He heard a rustling sound from within. He was sure he saw something move. There was the glint of a machete hanging off a nail in the shack, and he was afraid.

"I don't want to stay in here!" He turned to argue.

She pushed him, her palm on his face, and he fell to the center of the shack.

"Be quiet. Stay here," she hissed, and the last he saw was a big bright moon eclipsed by the closing door.

Outside, she bolted the door and looked to the house across the field. A light went on, and a white metal slat window began to roll open. Someone was looking her way; another problem to be dealt with, but first, the boy had to be quieted and secured.

"Stop whimpering," she whispered at the door. "I'll come get you tomorrow morning. Just eat a banana and go to sleep."

"Something bit me," the boy lamented, but she had already moved a rock in front of the door and moved away toward the house.

At San Juan's airport, the flight from Miami arrived that night and a heavy man, short and with sunglasses on, found his way to a car rental counter, selected a Toyota, and drove to a hotel nearby. He asked to be awakened early in the morning.

"Business?" the young man behind the counter asked.

"I'm meeting someone," the traveler answered.

"Ah," the young man murmured. He gave a wink to signify that he understood everything perfectly, though, in fact, nothing could have been more opaque, more hidden to him, than the motives of the man who stood before him.

CHAPTER TWO

Luis Gonzalo sat at his kitchen table, looking out through the white, metal slats of his window. Directly in front of him was the cup of coffee he had made for himself and the eggs and toast he had prepared. All of this had been done silently, without waking his wife or daughter. He had long ago come to understand that his occasional inability to stay asleep through to dawn did not constitute a sufficient cause to rouse the others in the house. But he wasn't just considerate of the others in his family. He also enjoyed the time to himself. Late nights and early mornings were the best time for thinking, and Luis Gonzalo thought of himself primarily as a thinking man.

Some disputed Gonzalo's estimation of himself. There were a

number of people in Angustias who thought he pretended to be an intellectual, throwing out a philosopher's phrase on occasion, liking classical music, going to Paris for vacation. To them, all these were just the airs put on by a man more proud than smart. Many of those who genuinely liked him did so exactly because he was not a thinking man in their eyes. He was good for singing a song or playing first base in softball or for helping to uproot a tree stump. They would have laughed if asked to think of their friend as an intellectual; after all, he didn't have a white beard or a tweed jacket or a smoking pipe. Even his own wife thought of him as something other than an intellectual. Mari always saw him as a man of great feeling, though she knew better than to accuse him of this to his face. Not that Gonzalo was particularly *machista*. But then, there was no reason to push the issue with him.

On this early morning—the sun was not yet beginning to peak over the hills of Angustias—on this morning Gonzalo was thinking of vapor. When he had rolled open the window and sat down to his coffee and toast, it was dark out. Now that he was finishing his breakfast, the first gleamings of sunshine were lighting the valley, and it became possible to see a cloud of morning mist beginning to slowly march its way up a hill a mile or two distant. "*March* may be the wrong word," he thought. It was almost as though an invisible hand were lifting the vapors up through the banana leaves and mango branches. Or as though a giant skirt hem were being raised, revealing the naked valleys of Angustias.

Gonzalo paused a moment in thought, the crust of a slice of toast between his lips. It appeared to him then that he had just solved a mystery that had perplexed him for years, not about the mist and morning dew but about a brutal assault on one of the citizens of Angustias. In that case, the man who had been beaten, Josue Perez, had refused to press charges or even complain of the beating he had so clearly suffered. The rising hemline of morning mist told Gonzalo all he needed to know about the attack. He was confirmed in his belief that one of Josue's drinking friends, Luis Salgado, had perpetrated the assault, and he finally came up with a motive for the crime and the victim's silence that made sense to him.

The two men had been in Colmado Ruiz, a grocery store that doubled as the only bar in Angustias, complete with pool tables near the checkout counter. Luis's girlfriend at the time was also in the store, playing pool while the men drank together. Gonzalo had considered that the fight might have been over her, but he had dismissed the idea. Flor Medina was too ugly for even a drunk to make a pass at her. That Luis Salgado was with her was a sign that what he felt was true love. But if the two men didn't fight over Flor, then what did they fight over? Both men had refused to say anything at all on the matter, as though Josue's nose weren't broken and bleeding and his left eye weren't swollen shut. They continued drinking together that night after Gonzalo had exhausted all his questions. All Flor had to say about the incident was that Luis had sent her to the pool table saying he had something to discuss with Josue. What the issue was was as much a mystery to her as it was to Gonzalo. He had left that night, unable to unravel the meaning of the fight and unable to arrest anyone for the obvious harm that had been done. It was only now, several years too late, that Gonzalo felt certain of the cause of the fight.

The two men had indeed fought over Flor, though she herself had no idea this was so. Flor was not sent to the pool tables so Luis could discuss something with Josue. Instead, she was sent in order to get a response from Josue as she leaned over the table in her miniskirt to make a shot. Luis Salgado wanted to make his friend salivate over Flor's legs. When Josue ignored the legs—thin and knobby— the fight started. The fact that Josue had refused to insult Flor with a catcall was an even greater insult in the drunken mind of Luis Salgado. Case closed. The solution drawn, literally, from thin air.

He turned his solution over in his mind, and thought of the utter futility of his deduction—Josue Perez had died in a car crash in San Juan two years earlier. A noise brought him back to the present. He swallowed the coffee he had already drawn through his lips and paused a moment. He wasn't sure he had heard the knock; it was so small. It came again, still barely audible but a bit stronger.

He checked the clock that formed part of the stove. As always, it read twelve o'clock. His own watch read 6:23 A.M. There was another knock, and he went to the door. As he undid the lock, he thought of how completely inappropriate it was for the sheriff of Angustias to be opening the door with no shirt on, with only a pair of dungaree shorts on and a pair of slippers. "Almost nude," he thought. And without even asking, "Who is it?"

The man on the other side of the door was known to Gonzalo in the same way most of the nine thousand citizens of Angustias were known to him: very well and for decades.

"*Entre, entre,*" Gonzalo said, opening the door wide. *Come in, come in.*

Tomas Villareal scurried into the house as though he were afraid the door might close on him again. At forty, Gonzalo was five years older than Tomas. This was part of the reason why he did not consider Tomas a friend, though he liked him enough as a person. In a small town, it can be a little difficult to make friends with someone if you haven't gone to school and shared classes with them. Still, the age difference was a small one and only made the friendship difficult, not impossible. Years, however, were not all that separated the two men. Tomas and his wife Isabel also seemed a bit alien to Gonzalo and the rest of Angustias.

The Villareals were two of the very few Protestants in town, and they were the only Protestants in Angustias who had been born as Catholics. They were the only *Angustiados* who publicly rejected the doctrines of the Holy Mother Church and embraced what most *Angustiados* called Luther's Curse. Except for two or three families who had inherited their Protestantism, all the other Protestants in Angustias had come from beyond the borders of town. Those from out of town had often insulted Angustias by claiming to be "Christian" missionaries. But those from outside of Angustias and those *Angustiados* who were born Protestant were seen as merely annoying or silly. The conversion of Tomas and Isabel five or six years earlier was treachery. They were seen as adults who had decided for themselves that all the rest of Angustias was wrong; every person in town felt judged by this decision. The ideas of those who were born into Protestantism could be accounted for as an inheritance. The beliefs of outsiders were always incomprehensible. But the conversion of Tomas and his wife could only be understood as a slap in the face of all those who had been their neighbors and friends since childhood. This conversion, as heartfelt and public as it had been, was the source of occasional small frictions between the Villareal family and the rest of town.

"Come in. Sit down. Sit. How can I help you?"

Gonzalo coaxed Tomas into a seat at the kitchen table. Tomas looked anxious and, though it was still a cool morning, he wiped the sweat off his forehead with the palm of his hand. He pulled out a chair and sat. He planted his feet on the ground and folded his legs under the table. He was something over six feet tall, so he was three, maybe four inches taller than Gonzalo. However, where Gonzalo might have been described as stocky, the only word for Tomas Villareal was skinny. When he rested his elbows on the table, Gonzalo could see that the short sleeves of his shirt were nearly empty, his bony arms not taking up much space at all. Gonzalo wondered for a moment whether Protestants were prohibited from eating pork.

"We can't find Samuel," Tomas blurted out.

Gonzalo sat thinking for a moment. People who sought him out usually beat around the bush a while, and he was preparing to make some small talk. He was going to start with an offer of coffee.

"Tell me more," he said.

"We went to wake him up for school—he's a second grader. He goes in at seven-thirty, he has to be at the bus stop at seven o'clock, it's a staggered schedule, but today is a . . ."

"There's a half day. I know the school schedule. Tell me about Samuel."

"He wasn't in his room. He wasn't in bed. We checked the whole house, the backyard, the shed, the property, everywhere. I don't know where else to look. I don't know who else to ask."

"Did you call the station house?"

"No. You're closer."

"Okay, but next time, go to whoever's on duty. Look at me. I don't even have socks on. Anyway, continue. When was the last time you saw the boy?"

"Last night."

"What time?"

"Pretty early. My wife and I went to a convention in Ponce. We left him and the girls around six o'clock."

"Convention?"

"Prayer convention."

"Oh. What time did you get home?"

"Around one."

"Midnight Mass?" Gonzalo asked.

Tomas squirmed a bit. Pentecostals don't celebrate Mass. He felt for a moment that Gonzalo should have known.

"Something like that," he said.

"Did you check on him when you got in?"

"No. I don't think so. I know I checked on Marisol."

"Which one is that?"

"The oldest girl. She was sound asleep. I didn't want to bother the other two kids. Besides, I was very tired."

"I understand. Was Marisol kind of in charge last night?"

"Yeah. She's fourteen. That's okay, isn't it? I thought she was mature enough to handle the boy and her little sister."

"It's fine, fine. But did you talk to her yet?"

"No. Not yet. She's in a rush to get ready for school. I didn't want to disturb her. Do you want me to tell her to stay and help us?"

"No, no. It's okay. Look. Let me tell you something. I'm not judging you. I'm not judging your parenting skills; I'm not judging your investigative skills. I'm just asking questions. I need information, that's all. No one is judging you, okay?"

"Not yet. People will, though. They'll say, 'See? Those Pentecostals can't raise their children right.' Some will even say that God is punishing us. . . ."

Gonzalo threw his head back and sighed. Of course, what Tomas said was all true. People would talk about Tomas and Isabel. Many would view their religion as a reason why the boy was lost. But in his eyes, all of that was plain foolishness and only a fool would listen to it. He thought for a moment of asking Tomas why he didn't just come back to the Church and avoid all future unpleasantness. But he knew the decision to change faiths had not been an easy one, even though he had no idea what exactly had been involved.

"Look. I can only give one piece of advice when it comes to people talking about you: Forget them. Don't even listen to them. Every parent goes through a scare like this. Ninety-nine times out of a hundred, it is completely harmless. Little boys wander off all the time. Hell, you know Doña Cambucha? Her youngest son, Tito, was one of my first cases almost twenty years ago. I looked everywhere for that boy. He was about eight or nine. Do you know how I found him? The sheriff of Aibonito called thirty hours after the boy was reported missing. He had simply gotten out of bed in the middle of the night and started walking. That's it. Just walking. He got fourteen miles away from here, caught frogs in a stream, was given food by strangers, while me and most of the town were searching through the woods and fields. I had a sore throat for two days after that from yelling the boy's name. Meanwhile, he was having a great time like a little Huck Finn."

"Who?" Tomas asked.

"Huckleberry Finn. Forget it. He's a character from an American novel—little boy who gets into a lot of trouble."

"Dennis the Menace?"

"Similar. Anyway, don't worry about what people say. If we're lucky, we'll find him in the next hour, and no one will know he was ever missing. If we can't find him before school starts, I'll talk to the principal . . ."

"He's the worst one of them all."

"Who? Martinez?"

"Him. He's an atheist."

"He's not an atheist."

"Of course he is. He's a communist."

"He's not a communist, he's a socialist."

"Same thing."

"Whatever. One way or the other, I know he's not an atheist. Anyway, if we don't find Samuel before school starts, I'll talk to Martinez and ask him to keep everything quiet in case one of the kids asks, okay? Now let's get out of here and start looking."

Gonzalo got up and started for his bedroom.

"Give me a minute, okay? Let me get some clothes on. We'll go see where Samuel has taken himself to. Start thinking of places he might have headed to."

Gonzalo padded carelessly to his bedroom. Once inside, he moved slowly and silently. All that he had said to Tomas had been in a calm, even tone. There was no point in getting Tomas any more excited than he already was.

Mari was awake in bed, lying on her side. He got into his trousers and sat on the bed to put on his socks and shoes.

"What's going on?" she asked.

"Samuelito Villareal, Tomas and Isabel's kid, is missing," he answered, tying a lace.

Mari raised herself to lean on an elbow.

"Missing? Since when?"

"I haven't really started the investigation yet. I'll ask more questions over there. I want to get a move on this. Parents are always nervous when they lose sight of their little ones."

"Of course. They should be. That's natural."

"I know. I've been anxious like that a few times, too, but Samuel will probably show up as soon as he gets tired of playing or hiding. He might be in his mother's arms right now."

"*Ay*, Luis. Don't be heartless. Have a little compassion."

"I'm having compassion," he said, and kissed her on the lips.

"I'm going out to find that boy without even finishing my coffee," he said, and slapped her rump.

The Villareals lived a few hundred yards away from Gonzalo, uphill and closer to town. Tomas had come over walking. Gonzalo decided to take his car. If Samuel had not returned home yet, he would need to drive into town and get the cooperation of his deputies. He insisted that Tomas climb in next to him, though Tomas wanted to walk back home and begin searching in earnest.

"Get in. I need to ask a few more questions."

Gonzalo's car was a dark blue Mitsubishi hatchback. He had had it for four or five years. He used it for official business more often than for private matters, and it had the mileage and wear and tear of a squad car. There was a dent on each side of the car, including its top side, and the windshield had a small crack. For some reason, Gonzalo could never understand why, the driver's side window never opened all the way, always leaving an inch or so of glass showing, making it impossible for him to rest his arm comfortably. More importantly, everything about the car squeaked so that he could not get in or out of it or even keep it in neutral without being heard. His chances of sneaking up on a suspect were slim.

Tomas sat with his knees flush against the glove compartment door.

"The chair goes back if you want."

"No, no, I'm fine."

"Okay."

Gonzalo put the car in drive and started up the hill.

"I wanted to know—have you or your wife had to reprimand Samuel recently?"

"Not recently, no."

"No spanking in the last week?"

They pulled up in front of the Villareal home. Isabel was on the front porch with her youngest daughter, a girl about the age of twelve. Gonzalo waited for the response in his seat.

"Let me see . . . I spanked Samuel last Saturday."

"Did you hit him hard? Did he cry?"

"Sure. No point in spanking him soft, is there?"

"No. But what'd he do?"

"Oh, let me see. He was using the refrigerator door as a swing. I told him to stop. He could break the door. He decided to keep on. When he swung on the door again, the refrigerator tilted. Lucky for him, I was there to hold it up; it could have fallen on him. As it was, everything in the fridge fell on the floor. There were bottles broken and food went everywhere. Isabel was cleaning up the rest of the day. I spanked him good for that. Why? You think he ran away for it?"

Gonzalo shrugged.

"You never know with kids. They don't always understand what's for their own good."

CHAPTER THREE

Like many houses in the main valley of Angustias, the Villareal family home was small, brightly colored, and made of concrete and cinder block. Their several acres rolled gently down and away from the back of the house for a hundred yards, then dropped at a breakneck rate for two hundred yards before leveling off in the area surrounding a stream that rode dangerously high right after a storm but was otherwise near dry.

One of the nice features of a house of this type is the compulsory porch, or *balcón*. The Villareal porch had a used sofa covered in plastic to go along with the usual two rocking chairs. There were also several large potted plants, something of an anomaly for the hills of Puerto Rico, where every house was surrounded by a thousand different plants. Another defining trait of the Villareal porch was the small, wooden doghouse sitting in one corner. Most of the *Angustiados* didn't think of providing a separate shelter for the dog to sleep in. As far as most were concerned, where the dog slept at night was none of their concern as long as it wasn't inside their own homes. In any event, the doghouse always made Gonzalo think the Villareal house was a little more picturesque than any other in that part of Angustias.

Isabel Villareal waited on this porch for Gonzalo to amble up to them. Her youngest daughter, Martha, was sent back inside by a command Gonzalo didn't hear. Skippy, a tiny cross between a Chihuahua and something not a Chihuahua, waited with the mother, alert, ready to attack. Gonzalo approached slowly, looking around carelessly, letting Tomas's long legs carry him to his wife. There was no point in rushing or appearing alarmed. In almost twenty years of police work, a hundred children had gone missing. One had been murdered, a little girl whose disappearance had been one of the first cases Gonzalo had dealt with; she had walked out of the tall grasses, bleeding her life away because of a savage rape by a predator Gonzalo had never caught, never forgotten, and never forgiven. Several other children had been found injured—a broken ankle, a broken elbow, cuts, bruises—rarely anything much to worry about. Only one child had gone unaccounted for in his years as sheriff, and most of the missing children by far had gone missing of their own will. He had little doubt but that this was the case with Samuel.

Tomas reached his wife while Gonzalo stopped a moment to admire a *flamboyán* tree growing at the side of the house. The bright red flowers were especially brilliant to his eye in contrast to the dullness of the young morning. From the corner of his eye, Gonzalo noticed Isabel hugging her husband over the porch railing. She cried bitterly but silently, and he would have liked to have stood with her and cried with her, but he knew that would have helped no one, least of all the boy. He stayed admiring the tree a moment longer, then paused a moment more. Rushing to the parents would only increase their anxiety. A few seconds alone with their grief would tire them, and they would be pliable to his liking and helpful in the investigation.

"*Dime lo que pasó,*" Gonzalo asked when he finally approached the parents. *Tell me what happened.*

"There's nothing to say," Isabel said, wiping her nose. "He left. I don't know where he is. I don't know where he could be. I don't know why or when. All I know is . . ." Here she choked back tears that threatened to drown her, and Gonzalo knew he hadn't waited nearly long enough.

"All I know is my baby is out there, maybe dead, and I don't know where he is."

Tomas looked to Gonzalo for some answer that could be made to such a self-accusation.

"Look," Gonzalo said. "There's no reason to get all broken up over your child right now. I guarantee you he's sitting under a tree eating *quenepas.* He's having the time of his life while you guys are crying your eyes out. He probably hasn't thought of you in an hour."

He paused to let the pleasant image of their son under a tree sink in.

"Now if we want to find him before the whole town starts looking for him, we have to put our heads together and answer some questions, okay?"

The parents nodded in agreement.

"Good. Now let's talk."

Gonzalo asked a series of questions and received one reply that he thought interesting. Samuel was fond of hiding in any shack with a hammock in it. He could sway forever in the quiet. Though he said nothing to Tomas and Isabel, Gonzalo believed that if the boy were feeling unloved because of a recent spanking, he might run away to the warm embrace of a loving hammock in the neighborhood.

This information might be useful, though almost every house in Angustias, and certainly every house in the Valley, had a hammock in a shack somewhere on the property. This practice was a holdover from a time when most of the *Angustiados* were farmers who needed to have a place to rest out of the noonday sun. It was one of the easiest traditions to maintain, as there has never been a generation that didn't fully understand the benefits of the hammock.

"Where are we going to begin looking?" Tomas asked. "We can't look in every shack in Angustias; there are thousands of them."

"We'll look in every shack if we have to," Gonzalo replied. "But that's not where we're going to start. First, I want you to drive down into the Valley as slow as you can go. Look around. If he ran away, he might have fallen asleep on the side of the road."

"I'll go with him," Isabel said.

"No. Someone has to stay behind in case he comes home. Now get your girls ready for school. They've missed the bus for sure; I'll take them."

"But what if he's walking uphill?" Isabel asked.

"The schools are uphill from here. I'll drive the girls slowly. Once I get them to school, I'll go into town and get my deputies. Don't worry. If he's still in Angustias, we'll find him."

Isabel looked at him with horror.

"What do you mean, 'If he's still in Angustias'?"

"Nothing. I meant nothing. Trust me. It would take hours for a child his age to walk out of Angustias from here. Even if he left last night, he would have fallen asleep long before he got out of town."

"But what if he was kidnapped?" Tomas asked, sharing in his wife's horror.

The question took Gonzalo somewhat by surprise. He had used so many comforting phrases in his ten-minute interview of the parents that he had forgotten that there might be real trouble in this case.

"He wasn't kidnapped," Gonzalo said. "Believe me. Nobody would drive all the way up to Angustias just to take the child of . . . excuse me . . . the child of poor parents."

"What about *Los Macheteros?* They take kids all the time," Tomas asked.

"Please!" Gonzalo begged. "We're wasting time here with pointless 'what ifs.' What if the Three Kings took Samuel? Let's stop talking and start moving."

The parents hesitated but agreed. Tomas got into his car and began driving deeper into the main valley in Angustias along the convoluted road that led to the next town, Comerio. Gonzalo could barely suppress a laugh as Tomas pulled out of his driveway at the side of the house at a speed of something less than a snail. Gonzalo signaled for him to quicken his pace while Doña Isabel went in to get her daughters ready for the trip to school.

In his own car, waiting for the girls to emerge from the house, Gonzalo thought about the possibility of abduction. It was silly and unproductive to waste energy pursuing the remote possibility that Samuel had been taken. Kidnappings are rare, so rare that they invariably make news even in cities like New York and London. He dismissed the idea that *Los Macheteros*—a violent, fringe political group seeking Puerto Rico's independence from the United States—

had anything to do with this kidnapping. Not that they hadn't abducted other innocents. It was just that they had left no calling card, no message, no demand. Gonzalo imagined that any group seeking to dramatize its cause would have made more noise.

Still, he knew he had misled the Villareals. Abduction was a possibility even if it was remote. Also, most abductions are not for money; many are motivated by a desire to hurt someone who is hated. He wondered if the Villareals had enemies who might go to such great lengths, stoop to such depths as to harm the boy just because he was the son of the wrong people.

The girls piled onto the backseat of his car. They both wore their public-school uniforms, but their skirts were an inch or two longer than usual. Both wore their hair in long ponytails; their hair had never been cut, and Gonzalo knew it never would be. Nor would they ever shave their legs. This was a strange requirement of their religion. They wore no earrings or other jewelry, and they never would until the day they were married. They wore the dull expressions of people who were doing as they were told. Gonzalo wondered about their religion a moment. Such loud, lively, even rowdy music during a church service, but lifeless at all other times. Strangeness notwithstanding, he couldn't think of anyone who would steal their child for that.

"How are you girls doing?" Gonzalo called out over his shoulder.

"Fine," was the response.

"Let's see. Martha, you're in the sixth grade, so you go to the *escuela elemental*. Marisol, you're fourteen, right?"

"Yeah."

"Then you're in *La Escuela Intermedia Eugenio María de Hostos*, right?"

40

The girl nodded to him in the rearview mirror. They drove on in silence another minute or two.

"Did either of you girls hear anything last night? Maybe you heard Samuel moving around late at night or something?"

Martha spoke up.

"We told Mami already. We each went to our rooms at nine, like always, right Marisol?"

Marisol nodded.

"I fell asleep, Marisol fell asleep. I thought Samuel fell asleep, too, but he must have stayed up. I guess he left in the middle of the night."

The girls looked at each other and nodded in agreement. Gonzalo pulled up in front of the junior high school and let Marisol out. She hugged her sister before leaving, then rushed to class. The eighth graders at Hostos junior high school started their day at seven o'clock, and it was nearly that hour.

The sixth graders at the elementary school started class at seven also, and it was a little past that hour when Gonzalo pulled up in front of the school to drop Martha off.

"Thank you," she said as she was about to close the car door.

"Martha."

She ducked her head back into the car.

"Are you sure you all went to sleep at nine?" he asked.

She looked to her shoes for a moment, then nodded yes, slammed the door, and walked off toward the school.

Gonzalo thought about her lie while making the U-turn to get back onto the road to the center of town. It wasn't just that it seemed unlikely that any children, no matter how well behaved, would go to sleep at their appointed bedtime when their parents were miles away and not expected for hours. He had already asked the parents, and they recalled that the doors to the house had been locked from within when they got home. Unless Samuel had a key to the house, the doors must have been locked while he was outside. No matter, Gonzalo thought. The girls are covering up for their carelessness. They forgot to check on him last night before locking up. Finding the doors locked, the poor boy most likely availed himself of the opportunity to go exploring and got lost. Gonzalo envisioned him huddled under some tree not too far from home, asleep after an exhausting night.

As he made his turn, a blue Toyota pulled up in front of the school, and the driver stopped to ask Martha a question.

"Hey, little girl," he called out in accented Spanish.

"Slow down. You're already late for class. Just answer me this."

Martha stopped for the man, though she could hear that the attendance had already been taken and the lesson had already started.

"Thank you," he said. "Could you just tell me when class lets out?"

"At twelve today," she said and started walking again.

"Wait. The little kids, too?" he asked.

She nodded her yes as she walked onto the school's playground and rushed on to class.

At the station house, Gonzalo found his younger deputy, Hector Pareda, on duty. In his two years on the force. Hector had grown on Gonzalo. He was young and intelligent, hard-working and loyal, if not exactly the most obedient deputy a sheriff could hope for. Hector was fond of racing other young men on the deserted nighttime roads of Angustias, though he was joining in on this activity far less often after several severe warnings from Gonzalo. He was also fond of a greater number of pretty young women than Gonzalo thought decorous for a police deputy. Gonzalo, however, tried to keep his opinion on this matter to himself as much as possible. After all, it was a handsome young man's prerogative to play the field and sow his oats. Still, every time Hector introduced another young lady, Gonzalo's left eyebrow raised to a degree that made the young lady uncomfortable and confirmed Hector's belief that Gonzalo had in fact never been young.

"What are you doing here?" Hector asked.

Gonzalo normally relieved him at a little before two in the afternoon. In this way, Hector watched the school children arrive in the morning, and Gonzalo saw the last group of children home in the afternoon. Since the school day was truncated, Hector was supposed to be in charge of watching both their coming and going. Gonzalo's day was supposed to be a relatively easy one.

"Samuel Villareal is missing. We've got to start some kind of search for him."

Hector sprang to his feet, anxious to get to work. This was another reason Gonzalo liked his deputy: Hector was energetic to the point where others exhausted themselves in watching him, and he was always up to doing any part of his job that didn't require him sitting and waiting.

"Where have you looked?"

"The Villareals started looking on their property. They tell me he's not on any part of their land."

"They checked the coffee shack on their property?"

"Yeah. I believe them. They've checked everywhere on their land. I think the boy walked off last night, and he's probably on one of the roads."

"Last night?" Hector asked. "I had in mind that he had left this morning. How do you know he left last night?"

"His parents said they were in church until late, and when they checked his room this morning, the bed was made. Anyway, let's get out there before the sun gets too high. I'm going to the Villareal house and walk through the woods in that neighborhood. I'll check my own property, etc. We'll let Collazo sleep through this one. The old man's been awake all night, okay?"

"Sure." Hector had relieved Emilio Collazo at six. Emilio was some fifty years older than Hector, though still very strong.

"I want you to drive up every road that branches off the main road in the Valley. Drive slowly. Take a good look around. Call out his name a few times, but not if you see people around," Gonzalo continued.

"Why not?"

"I'd like to find this child without people knowing that he's missing. There's no point in panicking the whole town if we can find him asleep under a tree."

"Panic? You mean you don't want people making fun of the Villareals."

"Okay. Whatever. Why should people make fun of parents who have a child missing? They haven't done anything. Anyway, let's get out there. I want to wrap this up as quickly as possible. It's no fun searching through the hills here with the sun beating down on you."

"Okay, chief," Hector said, strapping on his gun belt. "They say it's going up to ninety-two degrees today."

"Yeah? Who said that?" Gonzalo said, opening the door to the station house.

"Wilfredo Velez on WKAQ," Hector said as they left the building.

"That guy never knows what he's talking about."

"True. But it's going to be hot today. Believe it."

The two men walked to their separate cars. Hector was the only one of the peace officers in Angustias who drove the squad car. It was a powerful American-made car that slurped up a lot of gasoline, but he had altered it to make it even more powerful. He kept it as immaculate as his own car and got into philosophical arguments with Gonzalo about the value of having a high-profile vehicle prowling about the town. His argument was that if potential criminals saw him in a fast car, they would think twice about trying anything in Angustias. Gonzalo argued that the point was really moot. There was little in Angustias for potential criminals to do. The best way to stop criminals was to sneak up behind them in an unmarked, unremarkable car and surprise them as they were planning their crimes. Still, Gonzalo let him have the car with its lights and sirens. After all, Hector looked good in it.

CHAPTER FOUR

At about seven-thirty in the morning, or maybe a little more, Hector Pareda and Luis Gonzalo, two-thirds of the police force in Angustias, drove into the main valley of the town. The territory of Angustias encompasses most of three high hills and the two valleys that separate them. The valleys join to form a wider pass known to the *Angustiados* as *the* Valley. Among the three hills there are hundreds of gullies and hollows, folds and crevices, and in every cranny and nook in the territory of Angustias there is a house or two or three. While five thousand people choke the center of town, the four thousand remaining residents of Angustias live on the forty square miles that make up the outlying parts.

Hector enjoyed the job of racing up the various mountain roads, challenging the curves, and coming to a neat halt in front of an orange tree. Every few minutes in his exploration of the heart of Angustias, he got out of his car and surveyed the view, which became more magical the higher he went, and he called out Samuel's name. In half an hour he received only one response of any type. Though the cows ignored him, Julio Chagara could not. At a curve near Chagara's house, Hector got out of the car to call Samuel's name. Julio answered on the third call, standing only a foot or two behind the deputy, scaring him nearly off the side of the mountain.

"*Samuel no está,*" Julio said with the giant leaves of medicinal herbs plastered onto his face. *Samuel isn't here.*

" '*Samuel no está.*' What do you mean? Do you know who I'm looking for?" Hector asked.

"*Samuel no está.*" Julio repeated and walked away.

Julio had suffered from a severe case of meningitis as a child and had never matured mentally. It was common for him to speak in terms no one else could figure out; rarely did anyone try. "*Samuel no está*" could mean either that Samuel wasn't *there* or simply that Samuel wasn't at all. The difference, of course, was vast, but with a moment's reflection, Hector knew it would be worthless to press Julio for more information. The herbs on his face signified that Julio was trying to cure a pain in his head with a local remedy. There was no point in asking Julio much of anything when his head hurt; the pain (whether imagined or real no one could ever tell) interfered with already weak thought processes.

Hector cursed himself for having sustained even a second's hope that Julio could be useful to him, got into his car, and drove off. Though Julio had helped find several children in the last few years by driving through the countryside, the encounter with him somehow made Hector feel that the strategy wouldn't work this time. He drove a little faster than he had been, trying to leave this feeling behind.

Back on the main road after having dropped off both girls, the sheriff of Angustias was feeling sanguine about his chances of finding Samuel before noon. He entertained the idea that the boy might be walking into his mother's arms within the hour if he wasn't there already.

Gonzalo drove up to the Villareal home, where Isabel sat waiting on a rocking chair. Tomas's car was not in the driveway, and Gonzalo imagined that at the pace he left, it could be years before the car returned, possibly with the ghost of Tomas Villareal still at the wheel, patiently desperate and eternally sad.

Isabel bolted from the rocking chair the moment he turned off the car.

"Anything?" she asked.

Gonzalo paused a moment before answering. He knew the anxiety from which she spoke. Nothing he had to say would be a comfort.

"Not yet," he said. "We've only been looking for half an hour. Deputy Pareda is going up and down every road that comes off Interstate 157. We'll find him, don't you worry about that."

"No," she said sadly. "He's gone. Someone took him."

"There's no evidence of that. I told you. It's highly unlikely that anyone came all the way up here to take a child from poor people they don't know. You haven't received any threats, have you?"

"No. But he's never done this before. Samuel doesn't run away. He loves us. We love him. . . ."

"Look. There are a lot of things Samuel hasn't done before; he's only seven. Believe me, kids don't run away because they're hated. Most of the time, they have no reason at all. You have to be a bit stronger than this, Isabel. Tomas needs you to be strong for him, okay?"

Isabel sniffled a response.

"Good. Now I'm going to look through your house, okay? I want to see if there are any signs that he took things with him or that he had an idea of where he was heading, all right?"

Again, Isabel sniffled her response, and Gonzalo entered the house to begin his search, Isabel following close behind.

Though there were few Protestants in Angustias, Gonzalo had visited several of them. He knew not to expect crucifixes or portraits of Christ and the Virgin Mary. There would be no rosary hanging anywhere and certainly no candles unless for strictly utilitarian purposes.

The search of Samuel's room revealed little more than Gonzalo had already known. The bed had been made with care. There was an imprint on the blanket where Tomas had sat on the bed thinking a moment before going to get Gonzalo. The room was virtually devoid of toys, and Gonzalo wondered a moment whether it was religion or poverty that accounted for the deficiency.

A shirt was thrown in a corner. Gonzalo held it to his nose. It smelled heavily of childish sweat.

"It's the shirt he was wearing when we left yesterday," Isabel explained.

"Did he put on another one?"

"No. Not that I can see. I'm not sure I remember every shirt he had."

"I see his shoes and a pair of sneakers here. What's he wearing on his feet?"

"Sandals. They're black, made of rubber with nylon straps. They're for the beach, but he wears them everywhere."

Gonzalo moved next to the girls' room. Martha and Marisol shared bunk beds. Both beds were neatly made, and, in this room, nothing was out of place. The little bookcase was filled with study aids, textbooks, and Spanish translations of classic American children's literature, like *Little House on the Prairie* and *Little Women*.

"I wonder," Gonzalo said, upon pulling aside the curtain that closed off the room's closet. "Does Tomas have any idea that one of his daughters is using some of his shirts?"

Being the veteran of raising two daughters to adulthood, Gonzalo made a mental note to talk with Tomas about his girls once the boy was safe.

Only one other small oddity in the room attracted his attention: On the bureau, in plain sight, was a thin gold chain with a tiny gold cross, piled into a half handful. He thought to mention it to Isabel, but it would probably only get one of the girls in trouble, so he left it unmentioned and smiled inwardly that the girls showed more signs of normal adolescence than their parents would ever appreciate or understand.

"I'm done here," he announced.

"Anything?"

"Nothing useful. I'm just gonna take a quick look around your property to make sure he's not asleep or hiding in one of the buildings. You don't happen to have any old latrines on the property, do you?"

"I think we do. I think Tomas covered one up close to the property line with the Fernandezes. Why?"

"No real reason. Sometimes kids fall in . . ."

"Oh my God!"

"I didn't say Samuel had fallen in; I just said kids do that sometimes. Let me go check everything out, okay?"

The sun shone brightly into Gonzalo's face as he walked out the back door of the Villareal home and onto their land. The coolness of the morning was beginning to evaporate, and Gonzalo knew that soon the job of searching for the boy in the woods or on the highways was going to become irksome. As he strode past the manicured lawn and tended garden into the abandoned, wild growth, he thought that he would need to ask for help if he couldn't get some clues soon.

The outhouse was easy to find. It was a tiny structure, falling apart near the edge of the Villareal property. Inside, there were signs that the hole in the ground dug probably decades before the Villareals were born had been covered over with the trunks of banana trees. This was a poor job; even a child could move the dried, paperlike trunk of a banana tree, and children had moved them. Gonzalo aimed his flashlight onto the bottom of the latrine and found that a great many rocks and twigs had been tossed in along with a battered Barbie doll and a Tonka truck sitting at an angle that suggested a long struggle to climb up the wall of its purgatory.

Gonzalo headed next for the stream. For children, there is some terrible attraction to water. Beaches and ponds, pools and rivers are all fascinating to the young.

"Is it some kind of subconscious reversion to the womb?" Gonzalo wondered. Then he slipped.

Much of the soil in Angustias is hard-packed, red clay; even a small amount of water is enough to make this dirt as slippery as axle grease. When the morning dew hasn't completely dried off, the only way to descend a steep declination like the one behind the Villareal home is to secure footholds at the base of trees, moving from one tree to the next, holding on to vines and branches in between. Having practiced these moves since childhood, Gonzalo was able to make his way down much of the hill with great ease, but ease begets cockiness, and cockiness is father to carelessness.

The soles of Gonzalo's shoes had collected a cap of red mud, and when he stepped onto the enormous root of a mango tree, and shifted his weight without checking his footing, his leg shot out from under him so suddenly, so violently, he had pulled a muscle before he hit the ground. He landed on the root thigh-first so hard, he felt certain he had broken at least a bone if not his very soul.

He slid to a halt against the base of another tree about fifteen feet farther down the hill. He lay face-up on the ground for a moment with his eyes closed to better assess the damage he'd done to himself. When the shock of the fall had worn off and he was sure there was no broken thigh, he opened his eyes to find his pants torn where he had fallen and the seams of his shirt undone from the flailing attempt to stop his slide.

"Nothing broken," he muttered to himself. "But I certainly won't have to wait until morning for this to hurt me."

Gonzalo limped his way down the rest of the incline. When he reached the bottom, near the stream, he noticed a worn path zigzagging its way to the bottom. He made some comment to himself about how typical it was of him to find the safe way down after sliding nearly to his death.

Gonzalo found no evidence that anyone had been on that part of the Villareal property in recent days. But then, he wasn't looking as hard as he should have been. He was in pain and frustrated from his fall. Had he looked closely, he would have found some empty candy wrappers and a soda can with soda still in it. He would have noticed a rock near the stream with the moss cleaned off it and faint impressions in the grass around the rock. But Gonzalo wouldn't find any of this until later, until it was too late for a great many things. At that time his mind was much more on getting home, getting clean and into a new uniform than on the investigation. It would be too easy to blame him for that. You don't stop being human when you put on a badge. Sometimes the badge only adds official authority and weight to your mistakes and weaknesses. By day's end, Gonzalo and his deputies would have reasons to need to remind themselves of these things.

After a few quick turns near the stream, Gonzalo carefully made his way up the worn path and climbed into his car and drove the short distance home. Once there, he was assailed.

"My God, what happened to you?" Mari asked as he limped into the house.

"Fell down on the Villareal property."

"Are you hurt?" she asked, and he glared at her.

"I'm limping, aren't I?"

"All right, all right. No need to get snotty. I was just asking. Excuse me for caring. It won't happen again," Mari answered, picking out underclothes and a towel while Gonzalo limped to the bathroom.

"Carmen Fernandez called," his wife said.

"Great. What she want this time?"

"How am I supposed to know? She never leaves a message with me. She always has to talk to you personally. You're special."

"I'm not special; I just don't yell at her every time I speak to her. You're dragon lady to her; of course she'd rather talk to me," Gonzalo said, locking himself inside the bathroom.

Carmen Fernandez lived farther up out of the valley than the Villareals. Her family had been a pillar of the community when she was young, but she had always been in one kind of trouble or another.

"She is a woman of low values and loose morals," Mari said of her, and she was right. But Mari never investigated the reasons for Carmen Fernandez's behavior. She never sought out why Carmen early went with men, or why she hounded the good man who had married her to ulcers and to the grave, or why she abused her beautiful daughter, a thirteen-year-old gift from God who slaved away to keep the house in order under her mother's threats, or why Carmen Fernandez had spent nearly every night since the death of her husband drunk. "She is a woman of low values and loose morals." True, but these were symptoms merely. What the disease was, no one in Angustias knew, and no one cared.

The phone rang again just as Gonzalo stepped out of the bathroom in his underclothes. Mari answered the phone and waved him to her.

"Okay, Carmen. He's here. Just wait a bit."

Mari covered the mouthpiece with her hand.

"God, Luis. That bruise on your thigh is a foot long."

"I know," he said, taking the receiver.

"Doña Fernandez. How can I help you? Uh-huh. Okay. I'm looking for a child who has gotten lost, but I don't think I should . . . yes, since you know already, yes, it's Samuel. Oh. Are you sure? Since when? Are you sure? Okay. In about five minutes."

He hung up and took the uniform slacks Mari was offering him.

"Did she find Samuel?" Mari asked.

"Not quite."

"But she saw him?"

"Nope."

"Then what?" she asked, giving him a uniform shirt.

"Lydia Fernandez is missing. Carmen sent the girl out for a bottle last night, and she never came back."

"Oh my God!"

"That's right. Now I'm going over there to begin investigating; I need you to call Collazo. Get him out of bed. Get him over here. What time is it? 8:08. Great."

"You think the two kids got lost together?"

"I don't know, Mari. Maybe. I'll tell you one thing. The chances of two neighbor children deciding to run away separately at the same time have to be pretty bad," he said, putting on his shoes.

"But why would they run away together? They don't even play together," Mari asked. "What do they have in common?"

"That's what I'm asking myself. Anyway. Let me get out of here. Call Collazo." And Gonzalo went out the door.

CHAPTER FIVE

At the very summit of a high hill, there is a parcel of acreage fenced off from the wilderness that surrounds it. The area was supposed to be developed into some sort of radio station complete with tower, but the plan never became reality and no tower or station or other permanent structure has been built on the site, though the original fencing has had to be replaced because of rust.

In the fenced-in area, there were several windowless, wooden shacks, some close to crumbling. At first used for storing tools and supplies, now used for nothing at all, on the day of Samuel's disappearance, the day of Lydia's disappearance, there was activity in the largest shack. Three men were in the shack, one asleep on a stack of planks, the other two in close conversation. The man who slept, later described as having long, dark hair, was lean. To say he was thin would suggest a certain type of weakness that none who saw him ever thought to associate with his physique.

Many people saw the other two men, and the description of them is more complete. One man was young, in his twenties. He had dark hair also, but light skin. He was tall and everyone who remembered him remembered his thinness, and when they described him as thin, they meant to suggest a sort of thin-lipped, beady-eyed moral thinness. It was later found that he weighed something over two hundred pounds.

His partner in conversation was older, perhaps even sixty, not much more than five feet tall, and red. His hair was red where it was not fading to a blondish tone. His skin was certainly red, and it contrasted sharply with the broad gold chain he carried around his neck and the gold bracelet that made it just barely around his wrist. This last man was neither lean nor thin. He was fat. Though his shorts revealed legs thin enough to belong to either of the other men in the room, it would have been generous to describe this man as barrel-chested, to describe his hands as hammy. If one went to the trouble to describe these parts of him in this way, there remained the triple chin, which could not be euphemized so easily. Besides the gold jewelry he wore, there was also a pair of mirrored sunglasses so that only one man saw his eyes—they were bloodshot red. This was the man who had spoken to Martha Villareal as she entered her school playground.

"So when do we meet again?" the young man asked.

"When the deed is done."

"And we're sure it can all be done today?"

"The schools let out at twelve today. Plenty of time to get to San Juan and on a plane."

"But what if someone sees me? What if they chase me?"

"Who's going to notice you? It's not like you're grabbing a kid in broad daylight. It's not like he'll be kicking and screaming. You're offering candy. You have a puppy in the car. He'll be happy to go. You'll be one of many picking up children. You'll be back here before anyone notices. Heck, I might be on a plane before anyone even thinks about calling the police."

"I don't know . . . ," the young one said, holding his head with both hands.

"What don't you know?" the older man asked.

"You make it sound so easy. . . ."

"It is easy."

"Then why don't you pick up the kid?"

"Look at me. Do I look like I could be the father to a six-year-old? Hell, look at my hair. If I didn't wear a hat, I'd be spotted in a second. No. It's gotta be you."

"Yeah, okay. But what about the police?"

"In Puerto Rico? You've got to be kidding me. Learn this, my friend, and learn it well. There is no police force in any Spanish country that will do anything to an American citizen, especially not Puerto Rico. In any Spanish country, you can buy your way out of anything, out of murder if you have to, and the cops over here aren't like back in the States. Here, they're cheap."

"But I can't afford a bribe. . . ."

"Believe me. You won't need to. The cops over here are not that smart. No one's going to catch you." The fat man sat back and almost folded his arms across his chest.

"Okay. But what if one of the parents or a teacher follows me?"

"What if, what if. All these questions . . ."

"Any answers?"

"Yes. Look, don't take a tone with me, okay. I know what I'm doing. I have everything planned. You know how to get from the school to the Interstate, right?"

"Yeah. It's straight."

"And you know which way to turn, right?"

"Uh-huh."

"Right?"

"Yes. I have to turn left. Uphill."

"Good. And once you start uphill?"

"I know."

"Not good enough. I want to hear it."

"I get off on the third right, then straight uphill till I get here."

"Great, then your part is done, and you'll get your money in about a week. Five thousand, all cash. Then the fun begins for you. The guy wants the boy broken in; he wants him ready to perform. I tell you, that's the best part of all this. Our customer's some kind of sicko; he likes them young, but he wants them experienced. I say training them is the absolute best part. I would do it for that alone, forget the money. You never had a young kid, right?"

"You know who I've had."

"Raul? Raul was fourteen. Don't look at me like that, it's true. Swear to God. Fourteen years old. You thought he was ten, right? Well, that's why we come to these Spanish countries. The kids here don't develop the way American boys do. Over here they're late bloomers. A kid'll be sixteen without a hair on his chin. Look. Forget Raul. You're still a virgin. That's what we'll call you. You don't know anything yet. When you have had a young one, six, seven years old, then you know, then you're alive. Truly alive."

"That good, huh?"

"Listen to me. At first, the boys hate it. Of course. They don't understand. They think it's wrong; they went to Sunday school, whatever. That's fine. They don't know better. They hate vegetables, too. Then, in a few weeks, they accept it. I'm not saying they like it yet, but they figure it out. They say, 'So this is life. This is how it's going to be.' They get used to it. That's okay, but it's nothing special. But I'll tell you, just a little while after acceptance, something special happens. I tell you. There comes a time when this six-year-old, this seven-year-old, whatever, looks up into your eyes with such love in his eyes, such worship, such gratitude that you feel . . . you feel . . . look at me, I'm getting stiff just thinking about it. . . . I don't even know what it is you feel. Love is too weak to describe it."

"Wow. Really?"

"You'll see. Look. Why don't you cut your trip short and come home with me. You can see first-hand what I'm talking about."

"I can't. Really."

"Why not?"

"I'm traveling with someone."

"Yeah? Anyone I know?"

"I don't think so. No. I'm pretty sure you don't know them."

"Well, do you think it would be okay to meet this person? Do they like fish, too?"

"No!"

"What'd I say? What is it? You traveling with your mother?" The fat man laughed.

"No. It's my wife."

"Your wife? You're not married."

"I am now. I'm on my honeymoon."

"Your honeymoon? You sick bastard, you. Why didn't you say anything? I'd have given you something, a gift." The fat man laughed even harder.

"Well, you could give me the pictures back. . . ."

"What? You and Raul? Don't even joke about that. Those are my favorite ones. Wouldn't give those up for the world. Now look. You know what to do? You relaxed about all this?"

"Well, there's still one question you didn't answer."

"What's that?"

"What if someone follows me up here?"

"Okay. One more time. First of all, that's remote. Second, that car you're driving is brand new. Hell, you've seen 'em; some of these people still go on horseback. You saw the sheriff in his broken-down Mitsubishi. I don't think that car can go above fifty, and I doubt he has any deputies, okay? Still, if someone does decide to follow you, I'll be in my car. I'll be waiting. When you get off the Interstate, I'll be somewhere on the off road. I'll be watching you. If anyone chases you, they'll wind up in a little fender bender with me. Satisfied?"

"I guess."

"Good. Now get a little rest. There's about three hours before you have to be on your way to school. Besides, you have to be fresh for the little woman." The fat man laughed. "I've gotta meet her. Some women like boys, too," he said.

"Hey. You two planning to have kids?" the fat man asked. He walked off without waiting for a reply, laughing as he went to the latrine.

The young man sat a moment in silence. He had not thought of becoming a father before, and he wondered what to make of the proposition.

CHAPTER SIX

Going to the house of Carmen Fernandez was never fun. The first time Gonzalo responded to a call there, Carmen had been locked outside, enraged, drunk, and with a knife. She had then just found out that Ramon Fernandez, her husband, had committed the ultimate betrayal against her—he was dying of ulcers that perforated his stomach and upper intestine, forming small sacs of blood that ruptured violently when he vomited. If he would be so cruel as to die on her, she would kill him for the offense.

On other occasions, Gonzalo had gone over to investigate suspicions of child abuse harbored by Agustin Martinez, the elementary school principal. There was no evidence of egregious wrong being done to the girl, but the only reason Lydia wasn't removed from the house was that she had no other family to go to. The house was no home, the mother not truly a parent, the food was little more than candy, and discipline was capricious at best. Carmen Fernandez was rather more neglectful than abusive, and, in fact, it was becoming clear to the people of Angustias that it was now Lydia who cared for her mother rather than the other way around.

Carmen waited for Gonzalo outside her house, pacing and holding herself; several seconds passed before she noticed him. When she finally saw him standing before her, she paused a moment, then approached him with an upraised fist.

"She's gone!" she screamed, coming closer.

Gonzalo stood his ground. Somewhere in the back of his mind, he had the thought that he might have to take a punch to get useful information from her. In the front of his mind, he had no clear thought. Certainly, he couldn't run away from a woman, especially not a woman in such desperate need.

She didn't strike him.

"She left. She's gone. She ran away."

Gonzalo reminded himself not to show his true emotions. He was happy this was not a *Machetero* abduction. He was happy Lydia had only run away. Runaways often return, he knew, but it would have helped no one just then for him to smile.

"Okay. Calm down. Give me the details. Tell me what happened, okay?"

"There's nothing to say! What do I have to say?" Carmen yelled.

"Of course, there's something to say. You didn't call my house for nothing. You're not out here waiting for me for nothing. Come on. Take it from the top. When did she leave?"

"I was watching a *telenovela,* the one where the mother has two husbands . . ."

"Vivo por Elena."

"That's the one. When it was over, I sent her to Colmado Ruiz."

"That's more than a half mile away."

"So? She's young. She can walk."

"Okay. What did you send her for?"

"You know what for."

"Bacardi?"

"Why not? I'm an adult. Anyway, I sent her to the store when the show was over."

"Nine o'clock?"

"Yes."

"How much did you give her?"

"Huh?"

"Ten, twenty? How much did she have on her when she went to the store?"

"How am I supposed to know?"

"Did you give her money, or did you want her to get the bottle *fiao*?"

"What's the difference?" Carmen asked.

This was one of Gonzalo's pet peeves in police work. A large number of the culprits, victims, and witnesses he met every day were drunks who swerved on the road of questions he was trying to lead them on. Were they hiding something, or did they truly not know the answers to his questions? This was too often very difficult to decide. Due to the nature of this particular case, Gonzalo decided that Carmen Fernandez probably didn't understand the reason for the question.

"The difference is," he started slowly, "that if you gave her twenty dollars, she could have taken a cab to San Juan. If she had no money, she probably walked to a friend's house. See?"

Carmen Fernandez paused a moment. When not fully concentrating, she swayed as though she were tipsy, but she couldn't be drunk; she hadn't had a drink since the night before.

"I didn't give her anything."

"Good. Then she can't be too far away. Do you know if she took any clothes with her?"

"I don't know. You mean more than she was wearing?"

"Yeah."

"I don't know. I don't think so."

"Did you see her go?"

"Yeah."

"Did she have any bags on her?"

"I don't know. I don't think so."

"Good. Now, has she ever done anything like this before?"

"Like what?"

"Has Lydia ever run away from home, even for a few hours?"

"Oh. A few hours? Yeah, sure. Even I've run away from home for a few hours before. Doesn't everybody run away for a little while?"

Carmen's question was asked in a serious tone, but Gonzalo thought it best at the moment to refrain from preaching to her about responsibility and setting an example.

"Where does she go when she stays away from home?"

Carmen thought a moment before answering.

"I asked her once. She said she went to a hill where she could get a good view. She likes to sit where she can see the ocean. I told her the ocean was a waste of time. For that she could save the trouble and watch TV, but kids don't listen."

There were a limited number of places in Angustias where one could see the ocean and only one within walking distance of the

Fernandez home, so Gonzalo had hope that this might be a very easy case to solve. Still, he would cover all bases.

"Why didn't you call me last night? Why wait until this hour?"

"No special reason. I fell asleep. I woke up at midnight looking for the girl. I didn't find her. I fell asleep again; woke up at five. She still wasn't around; I looked for her outside. I looked for her out back. I called her school; Martinez said she wasn't there. That's when I called your home."

Gonzalo had his small notepad out and was scribbling in it, an activity that made Carmen anxious.

"Any friends that she could be staying with? Especially if the friend's parents are away or not too strict."

"No friends."

"Any friends in the neighborhood at all?"

"No friends at all."

"Not even the Villareal girls?"

"No friends at all. She hates the Villareal girls. Believe me. She thinks they're stuck up. I think so, too, if you want to know. No friends. I know. We have only each other."

Gonzalo looked at her with an eyebrow raised in doubt. Every mother believes she knows all the important details of her children's lives, and Gonzalo knew every mother was deluded in this regard. Even the youngest children may have secret lives that would amaze their parents to know.

"Anything else?"

"No, Doña Carmen. I'll just take a quick look in the girl's room, then I'll go out and start looking."

"Why do you want to look in there?" Carmen clutched her shirt up to her neck as though Gonzalo had suggested checking her bra.

"I might be able to find something that tells me what her plans are. Maybe a diary or a letter," Gonzalo said calmly, moving toward the house.

"Diary? That girl barely knows how to write. Believe me, you don't have to waste your time looking in my house."

She made a move as though to block his path.

"Are you hiding something, Carmen?"

She pondered the question a moment, then stepped aside quietly. Gonzalo walked to the door.

"It's a little messy inside," she yelled after him. "I haven't had a chance to clean up. I've been too worried."

Inside the house, there were bottles and dirty plates in unlikely places. Gonzalo noticed a newspaper dating back to the previous election some months before. The sofa faced the television, and there was a heavy blanket on it, along with a pillow. This apparently was where Carmen Fernandez had fallen asleep the night before.

Gonzalo's search of Lydia's room was only a cursory one. He was anxious to get out to the hills to find the girl's favorite lookout spot. The girl's room was also a mess, with clothes accumulated on the bed, the chairs, and even the top of the bureau. The bed hadn't been made neat in a great while, Gonzalo estimated. Perhaps never. The only thing that caught his interest at all was a thin gold chain with a tiny gold cross. Its similarity to the necklace he had seen in the Villareal house escaped him. Instead, he recalled that Lydia Fernandez wore the chain every day; he was sure he hadn't seen her without it these past few months. Yet, here it was, laid aside as though put off for the night. If she was proud of the chain, and she clearly was, and she was planning to run away, why wouldn't she take it with her? After a moment's pause, Gonzalo decided it would be better to solve this little mystery while looking for the girl.

Deputy Emilio Collazo was waiting outside when Gonzalo emerged from the house. He was leaning back against the side of his car, his arms folded across his chest.

"Anything?" he asked.

"Not much to go on here. Still, I think it might be an easy case. The girl ran away last night around nine o'clock—her mother sent her to the store for a bottle . . ."

"Some mother."

"Yeah, well, whatever. We're not here to judge Carmen; we're here to find the girl. Now, her mother says the girl goes to a hilltop to look at the ocean. Am I right if I say the only place she can go to see the sea from here is *La Torre?*"

Collazo thought a moment.

"Yup."

"Good. Then you can go to *La Torre* while I go talk to Agustin Martinez."

"Why am I going to *La Torre?* I doubt she spent the night outside. She can't still be there."

"No. But you might be able to find some signs that she was there. That would account for some of her time, it would tell us which direction she headed in. You could ask the people around there if they saw her, if they know where she's staying. Think about it."

"Okay. But I think you're forgetting something."

"What?"

"You can't see the ocean at night from anywhere in Angustias. I won't even mention the fact that all of *La Torre* is pitch dark at night. They don't have lampposts up there yet. If she tried walking up that way at night, chances are she broke a leg."

Whenever Gonzalo was working on a case, there was nothing more frustrating for him than to have to interact with and depend upon others. Others were not a true extension of himself; they didn't know what he was thinking or feel as he did. They argued with him and slowed him down—he was obliged to answer questions and explain every step of the investigation. One of the things that made Collazo a good deputy in the sheriff's eyes was that he rarely asked questions. In fact, Collazo spoke so little during an investigation that if there was independent thought going on, Gonzalo was almost never aware of it. Nothing could rile the sheriff more than a display of independent thought that led to a simple, common-sense conclusion he had overlooked. Even so, Gonzalo had learned long before that hurt pride was difficult to heal and best swallowed.

"You're right. Still, drive up to *La Torre* anyway. She might be there now. Take a quick look around."

"And if she's not there?"

"Then try to get me on the CB. Hopefully, I'll have some names of friends she might be staying with."

"Okay. What about the Villareal kid?" Collazo asked.

"I'll work on that. I'll talk to Agustin Martinez, see if I can get any information from him on either case. I'll get the list of friends. Then I'm going to continue the search for the boy."

"Not too worried about Lydia?"

"Nah," Gonzalo tossed over his shoulder on the way to his car. "Kids run away all the time. Ninety-nine-point-nine percent of them go back home in a day or two. Get to work."

With this, Gonzalo got into his car and drove off toward the school. Collazo headed for *La Torre*.

La Torre was one of the highest points in Angustias. The peak got its name from the fact that a member of the richest family in Angustias, the Mendoza family, had begun construction on a castle of Old World proportions at that height. The project was a logistical nightmare. A road was built to carry the men and materials. An acre of trees and underbrush was cleared away. Without the root system, the soil eroded in small mudslides whenever it stormed. What was left had to be leveled off and firmed up with the importation of stone and the construction of retaining walls. A foundation was laid, twice. Several sections of the castle were begun, and what looked like a tower complete with battlements could be seen from many parts of Angustias.

Construction was halted when Carlos Mendoza found that the woman he intended to be his queen in this castle was not interested in him. In fact, she thought him laughable and felt free to prove her disdain with a slap and a snigger. A toss of her hair and a turn on her heel and Carlos was left fit only for institutionalization. He had, in fact, only recently been released. Still, the views from *La Torre* are undeniably beautiful, and lovers have been going there for privacy since even before construction was halted.

Collazo found little of interest at *La Torre*. There were beer cans and soda cans, signs of several barbecues and paper plates. There was one sock, one sneaker, and one men's undershirt, all of which appeared to have been there for a year at least. There were cigarette butts and condom wrappers in abundance, and he found eighty-seven cents, which he collected. Of the building itself, there was little for Collazo to remark. Its most peculiar feature was a staircase standing in the middle of a large room, rising to a second story that was never started. Instead, with the right angle of vision, the staircase appeared to climb to the clouds above.

"Disgusting," Collazo thought. "This man's foolish pride has created a ruin useful only for the confusion of sins. A second Tower of Babel."

For Collazo, a strict Catholic all his life but even more so as he aged, the condom wrappers and beer bottles signaled premeditated drunkenness and debauchery.

"How can they confess these sins?" he thought. "How can they confess when they travel here with the purpose, the intention of doing wrong? When they will come back here with the same intentions after the confession? Who do they fool, and why do they bother to hide?"

Collazo took a final turn around the castle. From that point, he could see to the ocean on one side, to mountains on another side, and to cities far away elsewhere. He stared at the cities of the plains for a moment, thinking of them as Sodoms and Gomorrahs. He hoped they would feel the eyes of righteous indignation boring into them. He saw himself as a Biblical patriarch, complete with staff and tunic, ready to call down the wrath of God. Then he snorted out a laugh and turned back to his car.

"You're no Abraham, old man," he told himself. "Many of them may be wicked, but you live among them as a neighbor. If you wish them ill, then you have a wickedness of your own hiding inside.

"Hypocrite," he told himself as he got in the car. "If you look to your own life, you'll find enough flaws there to worry about."

He drove away to find Gonzalo.

In terms of gathering useful information, Gonzalo did little better than Collazo. Principal Martinez had little to tell him.

"What can I say? Samuelito is a well-adjusted, happy little boy. I never heard that he had any trouble at home even though his parents are a little strange. . . ."

"Strange, how?" Gonzalo asked, though he was sure of the answer already.

"Well, their religion. You know."

"Yes. Go on."

"Frankly, I would have thought his sisters were capable of running away. . . ."

"Why?"

"Well, they're at that age. Very difficult under any circumstances. Then, because of their religion, they don't quite fit in. . . ."

"Anyone ever threaten them? Harass them?"

"Oh, no, no. Nothing like that. It's just that there's a whole body of experiences that they don't share—First Communion, Confession, Mass—you see what I mean. Anyway, there's that on top of the usual storm and stress of becoming adults. Then there are hormones and the usual loves and hates associated with their ages."

"I see. Anything about Lydia?"

"Well, Lydia's a little slow to develop . . . mentally. She may not have an actual problem. Her home environment is not conducive to learning. She has some obvious reasons for wanting to leave home; though, again, she's as well-adjusted as can be expected under the circumstances."

"Any friends she might have gone to?"

"No. No friends that I've seen; no one particularly close. She keeps to herself most of the time. She goes straight home after school. She does have a boyfriend, whatever that means at her age."

"Boyfriend? How old is she?"

"Thirteen. She spent two years in the fourth grade. She's developing physically much faster than mentally."

"I see. Can I talk to the boy?"

"He's in the junior high school. Pedro Rios. Seventh grade, I think. He's a little stuck up."

Gonzalo wrote the boy's name into his notepad and tucked the pad into his breast pocket.

Outside, Collazo was waiting to make his report.

73

"Anything?"

"Nope. No sign of the girl at *La Torre;* just a lot of beer cans and such."

"Well, I got the name of Lydia's boyfriend—Pedro Rios, a seventh-grader. I'm going to pay him a visit."

"And me?"

"The girl has no friends, according to Martinez. Go help Hector. Start knocking on the doors near the Villareal house; the boy could be sleeping on someone's sofa."

"Every door or the ones where children live?"

"Every door. Kids his age will go anywhere there's a smile to greet them or a glass of soda to drink. Let's see. It's nine-twelve. I'm going to the junior high school. I'll try to catch you in the Valley by ten. Keep track of the houses you contact, okay? Good. Let's move."

Both men went to their cars and drove away from the school—Collazo to find Hector Pareda, Gonzalo to find Pedro Rios.

Pedro Rios was one of those teens who somehow reaches the conclusion that their years and personality, their looks and their smile make them of greater importance to the human population in general. This conceit is usually beat out of them by some other, larger teen before the seventh grade is done. Sometimes the child survives to high school age without having received the appropriate lessons, but this is rare. It doesn't often take so long for someone to act on the impulse to smack them.

Pedro's hair was slick, but unlike most of the boys in his class, it was combed back, not to the side. Though he was obliged to wear a yellow and blue uniform like all the other public school students, he would go home and change into better play clothes than most children wore to church.

Gonzalo spoke to Pedro outside, under a tree. The boy crossed his arms and gave the sheriff an insufferable grin that made him want to scare humility into the child by slapping cuffs on his girlish wrists or by simply slapping him. Gonzalo restrained himself.

"I want to talk to you about Lydia Fernandez."

The boy's grin disappeared, and he shuffled his feet.

"Did you meet her last night?"

Pedro's eyes widened in genuine surprise.

"No sir. I don't know who could have told you anything like that, but I've never met with her at night. I only talk to her after school, on the bus. The bus picks her up first at her school, and she saves a seat for me. Honest."

Gonzalo sized the boy up and decided he was telling the truth.

"Well, do you have any idea where she might be right now?"

"She should be in school."

"I know that. She's not in school. She's not home either. It looks like she ran away. Any idea where she might have gone?"

"No sir. If she's not home, I don't know where she is. She doesn't have too many friends."

"Does she have any friends?"

"Just me, I think. She doesn't have time for friends; she has to go home right after school most of the time."

"That must get a little boring for you as her 'boyfriend.' When was the last time you spoke with her?"

Pedro looked to his feet and began to swing his arms.

"I haven't spoken to her really in a week or two."

"Why not?"

The boy shuffled his feet some more.

"I kinda lost interest in her. There's another girl I like better. You know how it is." He smiled in Gonzalo's face.

"No. I don't know. How do you think this makes Lydia feel?" His look of disgust killed the little boy's grin.

Pedro had no answer so he looked to his shoes again. He had obviously never considered that Lydia might feel anything at all; at least not anything of importance to him.

Gonzalo walked the boy back to his class, then walked to his car. It was 9:45 A.M.

CHAPTER SEVEN

Most of the people of Angustias thought of Mari Gonzalo as her husband's partner even when it came to police work. Many would come to her to report their troubles—an abusive husband, an employee suspected of theft, a missing animal—and they expected her to get to work in providing solutions. Of course, she tried her best to help; these people were neighbors. But she also handed these problems over to her husband. As she sometimes had to remind the people who came to her door, she wasn't the sheriff or a deputy. She had no legal authority or special expertise to help them, no matter how much she sympathized. Besides, there was always laundry to do or floors to mop; there was a young child to care for and two older ones to watch from a distance. If she stopped to solve the problems of the world, these things would not get done. Certainly, Gonzalo wasn't going to do them.

Still, when there was a true emergency, Mari was more than willing and very able to help. This she would have done even if Gonzalo were not the sheriff. It was part of her nature to rise to each occasion, and the more daunting the occasion, the grander she rose. She had developed several strategies for dealing with the people affected by the accidents and crimes her husband investigated. She had been righteously indignant with a mother who blamed Gonzalo for arresting her criminal child. She kept a room ready for people who were too afraid to return to their own homes. For the many anxious people who came to her door, those for whom the hospital visiting hours were not long enough or whose little children were missing, for these, Mari had food and chores.

Years before, she had learned that the anxious mind often needed nothing more than to think of something else, anything else, however trivial. Food was a good distraction. Many of the anxious had forgotten to eat. When crackers and cheese or rice and beans were put in front of them, they remembered hunger; they ate, and for a while forgot their troubles. Blood rushes to a full belly, away from a worried mind, easing digestion and relieving the brain at the same time. At least once a year, the spouse of a crime victim would fall asleep on Mari's sofa after hours of pacing and hand-wringing in a hospital.

Small chores also made them forget their problems, and they got work done. Children fed chickens, men might sometimes pick coffee, and women often folded clothes or dusted. One woman, in fact, contemplating the murder of her husband's lover, had mopped vigorously enough to snap the mop head off its wooden handle.

On this day, when Isabel Villareal came to the door after her husband had come home from his drive through the Valley, Mari put all other things aside for her neighbor and lent her ear to the outpourings of the desperate mother.

Mari greeted her familiarly. Isabel Villareal was not the first mother to come to the Gonzalo home in the early morning or late at night seeking comfort for an inward pain. As the sheriff's wife, Mari understood her job to include a fair amount of hand-holding.

"Isabel. Come in, come in. I was about to make some coffee. Do you want any?"

"No. No coffee, thank you." Isabel had already knit her brow into a knot and was wringing her hands raw as she walked through the door.

"Not even enough to keep me company?" Mari asked, trying to get Isabel to think of someone not herself.

"Oh. Sure. If you like. Half a cup?"

The two women went into the kitchen and began their preparations.

"Could you wash that pot for me while I get out the coffee and milk? Gonzalo makes his own coffee in the morning, which is good for me, but he always leaves a mess."

Isabel began the process of washing the pot and cup she found in the sink.

"Tomas came back from his search."

"Really? Do you take your coffee with a lot of milk or a little?"

"A little. He says he didn't see anything. He asked several people if they had seen Samuel."

"Oh? Do you want crackers with your coffee?"

"Sure. Nobody saw him."

"Samuel?"

"Right. Nobody saw him last night."

"Well, that's to be expected. Do you want some *queso blanco*?"

"Sure. They say they didn't see him, but I wonder."

"What do you wonder? Coffee's done. Let me have that cup."

"Not that much. Okay. I just wonder."

The ladies moved their cups to the dining-room table and sat to their small breakfast.

"What do you wonder?"

"I wonder if they're telling the truth."

"You think people would lie to your husband about Samuel? Why?"

"I don't think most people like us. Probably our religion."

"No, no. You're telling me reasons why they would lie. I meant, why are you suspicious of them? See the difference?"

"No."

"Well, what you're telling me is that they would lie because they don't like you. That's obvious. That's a reason anyone would lie to anyone else. What I want to know is what makes you believe that the information they gave your husband is false. By believing that they are lying, you are also saying that they should have seen Samuel. What makes you so sure? Why have you ruled out the possibility that Samuel simply did not walk in that direction?"

Isabel finished chewing on a piece of cheese before responding.

"I don't know," she said. Confusion was another way to distract an otherwise frantic person. "Well, maybe Samuel didn't pass through there. Tomas is going to go back out searching in the other direction. It's just that . . ."

"It's just that maybe you should not be so quick to suspect your neighbors. I know everyone in town. I have delivered babies and gone to weddings and funerals since I married Gonzalo and moved here. There are few I would say who would hold back that kind of information under any circumstances. Trust them a little more. If they say they didn't see him, it's probably because they didn't."

"But they hate us. You know that. Almost the whole town hates us because of our religion. This is not a secret."

"First of all, you're wrong. Secondly, this whole issue is really unimportant. There is plenty of reason for you to trust your neighbors."

"How am I wrong?"

"People don't hate you. I doubt anyone thinks of you negatively when they think of you. When they think of you, I'm sure they think your family is strange, but it's a long way from thinking you're strange to hating you. In fact, it's a long way from hating you to harming your child. Believe me. I've heard people at Christmas and Easter, at *las fiestas patronales*. There are people who miss you at church."

"They ask about me?"

"By name. They're concerned. They ask me how you're doing. These are the people you think are hiding information from you."

Isabel sipped her coffee, letting the seconds glide by as she thought. Knowing some town people still thought of her was nice, but her missing child only left the forefront of her mind for a moment.

"So if the people downhill didn't see him . . . I mean if we assume Samuel didn't go downhill, then that leaves uphill, right? He might have gone up the hill, toward Colmado Ruiz, right?"

Mari gave her response serious thought. On the one hand, it was better to have Isabel enthused about the search for Samuel than depressed. On the other hand, Mari could sense that a request to be driven up the hill, stopping at every door, was coming. While she certainly wanted the boy to be found, she also wanted to put the towels to wash.

"You know. He might not have gone along the road at all. He might have gone into the woods."

"Of course. You're right. I should have thought of that. Samuel may simply be lost in the woods. There are hundreds of acres in this area. He could be anywhere and no one would know it. I've got to find him. I've got to start now. I'll look everywhere. I grew up in this area. I played in all of these woods. Will you go with me?"

Isabel looked at Mari with such a great deal of hope in her eyes that saying "no" was impossible. The towels would have to wait.

"Sure. Why not? Just let me get some boots on," Mari said. She laced her boots slowly, hoping each second that Gonzalo would call. When he didn't, she walked out to the porch where Isabel was waiting for her.

"Where do you want to start looking?" Mari asked.

"Well, your husband searched my property and that area, but he didn't look on the lands across the road. Maybe we could start there." Isabel looked hopeful.

"Sure. Why not?" Mari answered, though she could think of several reasons.

The land across the road from the Villareal home was particularly forbidding. The underbrush was dense; the trees were uncared for, and the vines that smothered their branches formed an impenetrable canopy. After fifty yards of this type of territory, there were twenty feet of near-vertical rise. They would climb this by pulling themselves up, using vines and sturdy plants. When they finally reached a clearing, it would be crowded with six-foot-tall grass with sharp, cutting leaves. The stalks of these plants had tiny filaments that buried themselves under the skin of anyone who carelessly tried to make their way through the field. All this on a day that was already beginning to be too hot. Mari thought of complaining, of dissuading the mother who was clearly grasping at straws. Then she thought to herself that it was just this type of impossible terrain that would attract a six-year-old boy explorer. So they went.

Mari and Isabel first walked uphill to the Villareal home. There, Tomas was waiting for his wife on the porch.

"I've been waiting for you. Where have you been? You know we can't leave the phone alone. Someone could call at any minute."

Tomas's nostrils were flaring, and he was clearly very angry that his wife had taken as long as she had. Mari wondered whether Protestants beat their wives; probably no more than Catholics did, she concluded.

"I'm sorry. I . . . ," Isabel started, but she broke down and began wiping her eyes with her sleeve.

"I . . . ," she tried to continue.

Tomas also began to tear, and he reached for his wife with such a look of tired sadness that Mari was certain that if Protestants did beat their wives, Tomas, at least, was not a good Protestant in this respect. He cradled her, head and shoulders, holding her close to his chest and kissing the top of her head. Mari wished she were anyplace where this scene was not visible. It was the kind of pathos that can never be comfortable for those viewing it.

It was agreed between wife and husband that Mari and Isabel would search the woods an hour while Tomas stayed home. He could use the rest, and Isabel had energy that needed to be spent before she could be calm.

The first small hurdle to searching the property across from the Villareals was to duck through a two-strand barbwire fence and hop across a three-foot-wide drainage ditch. Isabel reached the other side of this in a squatting position, and her knees cracked loud enough for Mari to hear.

"*Mi'ja.* How long has it been since you played in these woods?" Mari asked.

Isabel glared at her.

The two women walked a parallel course within sight of each other. They made their way through the forest quickly, breaking their silence only to yell out the boy's name. Neither found any sign that the woods had recently been disturbed. They left the cool of the shaded area and entered a small clearing of chest-high grass. The entire walk until then had been sloping upward, but before them there was a sharp, unwooded rise. This lump upon the face of the Earth stood only twenty feet high, but it was a quarter-mile walk around it. The ladies rested a moment.

"Unless you've seen something, there is no sign Samuel came this way," Mari said.

This was clearly an invitation to give up the search, and Isabel had been thinking of this option before Mari said anything, but how could she give up so soon? How could she surrender without having first been defeated? Isabel could not see that her search was an ill-conceived waste of energy, no better than sitting by the phone at home. She was already frustrated near to tears, but she couldn't concede that maternity had not given her a divining rod for finding her son, that she was human, weak, and frail, even if her son needed something more than that right now. Tears welled in her eyes, and she tried to swallow a knot in her throat as she thought of these things.

"Go home if you're tired," she choked out at Mari.

Isabel attacked the hillside with a grunt. She clung to a fistful of grass and scurried her way up a few feet, kicking and dragging herself up the hill on her belly. She got a foothold at the base of a sapling and grabbed a rock farther ahead. Another clump of grass gave her a place to put her foot, and she took hold of an inch-thick vine above her and pulled herself up so that the vine was at her chin. She dug into the clay dirt with her toe; she made an inch-deep impression in the hill and rested. She was only ten feet from where she had started, and her arms were beginning to ache. Above her, she saw nothing but the stalks of grass and dirt. Below her, Mari was waiting patiently, holding on to a clump of grass.

Isabel let go with one hand to reach a point farther up the vine. Her toehold eroded beneath her. Her full weight pulled on the vine, and it snapped. On her way down the hillside, Isabel knocked Mari off. They landed in a tangle, the heel of Isabel's right foot thumping the back of Mari's head. Mari shook herself off before sitting up.

"That was very Three Stooges. Let's do it again," she said, holding her head.

Isabel, sitting with her knees up and her head in her hands, said nothing.

"Come on," Mari said. "I don't think I broke every bone that time."

"It's not funny!" Isabel cried. "Can't you see it's not funny? I'm a mother, and I can't even tell you where my boy is. Maybe I'll never see him again. I can't . . . I don't have the strength to climb even this little hill for Samuel. Maybe he's dying right now, and I'm too weak to help him. It's not funny! He could die because of me."

Isabel sobbed and choked on her tears. She found it difficult to get air into her lungs, and it came in gasps. Mari crawled over to her and held her, encouraging her to cry with pats on the back. She said nothing. What was there to say? Only one thing in the world interested Isabel, and Mari could give no guarantees that the boy was safe.

It was a little after nine-thirty when the two women walked out of the woods again and Isabel replaced her husband on the porch, waiting for the phone to ring. Mari headed to her own house, saying she would return after she had bathed and changed.

Instead, a few minutes later, Isabel watched her drive by in her car toward town. Mari didn't turn to wave or smile as she passed; she just drove, studying the road before her as though she expected it to change on her.

CHAPTER EIGHT

After talking with the boy, Pedro Rios, Gonzalo sat in his car in front of the school a moment. He put his head back against the headrest, pressing hard, trying to relieve the tension building up in the muscles at the back of his neck. The investigations of the day were not going as he had hoped.

"What kind of leads do I have?" he asked himself. "I started the morning with one lost child, and now I have two. I started out thinking that I could wrap up these investigations quickly and quietly. Now I'm just hoping I can wrap up these investigations at all."

He turned on the car.

"I can't start thinking negatively. The kids are in Angustias somewhere; I'm positive of that. Still, this is no longer a quick investigation. And if I have to knock on every door, it won't be very quiet for long."

He idled the car a moment longer and thought about asking for help.

When getting help from the neighboring towns, there were two options. The first option was to contact the sheriff of Comerio, a town large enough for its own mall a few miles south of central Angustias. Sheriff Molina was a Marine veteran of the Korean War, perhaps the only soldier who was sorry to see the police action come to an end. Violence was Molina's preferred language and currency. He was built along football player lines—his head embedded into his shoulders without the formality of a discernible neck. His arms could be described as "beefy" only if one meant to evoke the massive muscles of a bull's shoulder. The few career criminals of Comerio knew it was better to be charged with some crime if arrested than to be "questioned." There was some protection in having to pass under the eye of a judge.

The second option was to request assistance from the sheriff of Naranjito, a town to the northwest of Angustias. Susana Ortiz was young and beautiful; these were the most important strikes against her. She was also intelligent, which didn't help matters either. Finally, she was unmarried, so no one could help but think nasty things of her. Clearly, she was looking for trouble.

Susana was twenty-seven years old and had become a deputy upon graduating from college five years earlier. She had been sheriff for the last year and a half. There had been six other deputies who applied for the job, but only her application remained when it was made clear that the job included payroll mathematics. One might imagine a certain amount of resentment directed toward her, but resentment is hard to maintain against the disarming, and Susana was disarming in several ways. In the first place, she was tall (did her sin know no bounds?), taller than Gonzalo, which was an annoyance to him but attractive to many others.

She was also disarmingly shaped and did nothing with her uniform to hide this fact. She also did nothing to advertise her body, but this omission absolved her of nothing. After all, how were mothers to feel when young boys entering their teenage years did things in town with the express purpose of getting arrested or reprimanded or at least noticed by the sheriff and her hips? One couldn't very well blame the boys for noticing her.

The fact that she was also disarmingly witty, however, enabled her to win over even women of her own age, her most persistent detractors. On every occasion Gonzalo had had to work with her, she had been ready with some clever observation to break the back of tension.

These then were Gonzalo's options—he could call on Molina, a sheriff who was rather more brutal than intelligent, more vicious than useful—a man Gonzalo found difficult to work with. Or he could ask Susana Ortiz for help and not hear the end of it from his wife for some weeks to come. Knowing Mari's temper and how it could simmer indefinitely, he leaned toward calling on Molina.

"Or maybe no one," he told himself. "I'm not desperate yet."

He began to pull out onto the road when Mari parked her own car behind his Mitsubishi and honked at him. He put his car back into Park and got out, walking to her window.

"What now?" he asked. "Don't tell me there's another kid missing. . . ."

"Not in Angustias. In Aibonito. Two kids."

"You're joking."

"No. Last night, two kids walking home from a store were

picked up off the street and shoved into a van. They were gone before the witnesses could get a description."

"Who . . . ?"

"*Los Macheteros.* They called for a ransom. They called the mayor of Comerio with a threat. The mayor called Jorge Nuñez to warn us here. They're planning to take more children, they told him."

"Molina knows?"

"Knows? He closed down the schools already. His deputies escorted each child home. No child stays in a house alone. If the parents weren't home, the deputies brought them back to school. Every kid will be accounted for within the hour, he says."

"You're kidding me."

"Gonzalo. Look into my eyes. You see anything that tells you I'm joking?"

Gonzalo looked into her eyes briefly; they were filled with an angry seriousness that assured him she was telling the truth.

"Anything else I should know?" he asked.

"Only that *Los Macheteros* said the two kids would be dead by twelve if the money they want isn't delivered."

"How much do they want?"

"A million dollars."

"A million dollars! Aibonito can't even pay to keep the fountain running in their plaza. Where're they going to get a million dollars?"

"Not from them. From the government."

"¿*Los Federales?* They won't pay. Why even bother with them? Reagan said it: 'We will not negotiate with terrorists.' What's the point?"

"Don't tell me Gonzalo the Great can't figure it out. It's a no-lose situation for them. Either they get the money or they make the government look like they don't care about Puerto Rican children. Either way, they win."

"*Ay*, politics!" he spat out. "I hate politics; it's so dirty."

He ran his hand through his hair.

"Anything else?"

"No. I'm going to pick the girls up from school."

Gonzalo glanced at the back seat where their youngest daughter, Sonia, was strapped into her car seat.

"Why?" he asked, but Mari gave him a look that told him not to interfere with the protection of their children.

"Don't worry," she said. "I'll still be useful to you. I'll just drop them off at your mother's."

Mari drove away to the elementary school. Gonzalo walked back to his car slowly, as if in a daze. The entire complexion of his investigation had been changed by this three-minute talk with his wife. It now seemed more likely than not that the children had been taken by force. *Los Macheteros* were a small terrorist group dedicated to gaining Puerto Rico's independence from the United States. In the late seventies and early eighties, they had carried out several kidnappings and several bank robberies, and set fire to a row of American fighter planes. While their plans often went awry, Gonzalo knew they would not hesitate to do violence. He knew Mari was right— for fanatics, the kidnapping of little children was a no-lose situation.

Once in his car, Gonzalo drove straight to the station house at the center of town. There would be no avoiding the call for outside help, and with Sheriff Molina busy defending the children of his town, the call would have to be to Susana Ortiz.

The station house was a squat rectangle of a building attached as a late afterthought to the back of the *Alcaldía,* the seat of government in Angustias for 250 years. The building was small, but Gonzalo dreaded expansion. The only plan proposed so far was to knock out one of the walls and widen the building by a dozen feet or so. Everyone who had a vote in the city council favored this plan as the most economical except himself. Gonzalo opposed it as the most disruptive of his routine; he worried that they might knock the wall out and run out of money to finish the project. A jail cell with a missing wall would not be as useful as the cramped quarters of the current building.

When Gonzalo got inside the station house, Jorge Nuñez, the deputy mayor of Angustias, was inside already, sitting at his desk, speaking on the phone. He held up a finger to keep Gonzalo from interrupting his conversation.

"Ah-ha, ah-ha. Okay. Yes. Whatever you can do. Okay. Good. I'll see you soon."

He hung up and turned to Gonzalo.

"Susana Ortiz will be coming over with two of her deputies to help us look for the missing kids for an hour or two."

"That's great. I just heard about what happened in Aibonito. . . ."

"Me too, but you know what I find strange, Gonzalo?"

Gonzalo didn't know.

"I find it strange that I, the deputy mayor of Angustias, just found out about the children missing in my own town from a third party. Somebody who lives in the Valley called to ask me about the missing children; I told the truth, I said this was the first I heard about it. What I want to know is if there is any good reason why I should hear about children missing in Aibonito before I'm informed of children missing in my own town."

Jorge Nuñez was normally such a mild-mannered man that most of the town assumed he was kept as deputy mayor to counteract the painful brusqueness of the mayor of Angustias. On this occasion, however, he was clearly choking with anger. Having never seen Jorge so angry, Gonzalo felt at a loss as to how to explain himself. He felt suddenly guilty, though he knew he had intended no wrong.

"Nuñez, I . . . I . . ."

"Let me guess. You figured that since Ramirez was away, there was no one in a position of real authority. . . ."

"No . . ."

"Well, that's what it looks like, Gonzalo. Let me just remind you, in case you forgot, when Ramirez isn't here, I act as the mayor. If children go missing, I expect you to call your deputies first, and me right after them. You understand me?"

"Yes, but . . ."

"Good. Now tell me what you've done to locate these children."

"Okay, but let me say, Jorge, I meant no disrespect. I'm sorry, but let me explain . . ."

"Apology accepted. Explanation is not needed. Let's get to work. From now on, I want to know everything, okay?"

"Sure."

And Gonzalo informed Jorge Nuñez of what he had done and had his deputies doing since daybreak. He had just finished repeating the events of the day, checking what Mari had told him against the deputy mayor's memory, when the door to the station house opened and Susana Ortiz walked in.

"So you think it might have been *Los Macheteros*?" Nuñez asked.

"I think it's beginning to look like it might have been. I would never have suspected it if it hadn't been for the news I just got," Gonzalo replied.

The two men suspended their conversation to welcome the sheriff of Naranjito.

"I got news over the CB on the way over here. I don't think you guys have heard this yet. There was a child abducted in Morovis this morning. *Los Macheteros,*" she said, leaning back against the doors she had just closed behind herself.

The men looked to the ground in stunned silence. There seemed to them to be a clear pattern, and the children missing in their town seemed to fit into it neatly. In the minds of both men, *Machetero* involvement meant near certain death for the children—the ransom was unpayable and the abductors had not stopped at killing children in the past.

"Still," Susana broke the silence. "There does seem to be one piece of good news."

The men looked to her, encouraged.

"If I'm not mistaken, there hasn't been a ransom demand or a threat in Angustias, right?"

"Right," Nuñez answered.

"Then maybe there's no *Machetero* involvement. After all, killing a child without a ransom demand or a threat isn't a political act. It's just murder then. I figure if they don't contact Ramirez soon, they probably have nothing to do with these children missing."

"But how would they contact Ramirez?" Gonzalo asked.

"By phone, I guess."

"But Ramirez is in New York with his family. Even I don't have his hotel number. His house is empty. They may have been trying to call since yesterday for all we know," Nuñez said.

It was Susana's turn to stand in silent thought.

"Well, we can't worry about that now. The way I see it, we have to secure all the children, get the FBI involved, and begin a search for the unaccounted children," she finally said.

"Okay," Jorge said. "The children are accounted for, and we are already searching for the missing kids, but do we have to involve the FBI?"

"Of course. What if the kids are already in San Juan or Mexico or Miami? You guys need *Los Federales.*"

"Susana's right. They have information, names, descriptions, that might be helpful to us. If *Los Macheteros* are involved, we need help from outside," Gonzalo added.

"But they get in the way of everything, don't they?" Jorge asked.

"Usually," Susana answered. "But it'll take them an hour to find Angustias. With any luck, the kids'll be safe by then."

The three of them stood in silence. Jorge Nuñez looked to the ground, developing the course of action in his mind before speaking; as opposed to Mayor Ramirez, slow deliberation was the norm for the deputy mayor.

"I'll call the FBI office in San Juan. Gonzalo, you can deputize as many citizens as you think you'll need to conduct a complete search of every place those kids could be hiding. Just remember, of course, they should be trustworthy people who won't start any kind of panic."

"Sure. I'll probably be choosing a half-dozen people or so."

"Good enough. Use more if you need to. Sheriff Ortiz, I want to thank you for showing up here in our time of need. I guarantee you Naranjito will find a true friend in the city of Angustias whenever, God forbid, the situations are reversed and your city finds itself in difficulties. How long can your men stay at the schools?"

"Well, I'm sorry to say that our schools are also closing at noon. We have to be at full strength to escort the buses home. I'll tell them to begin making their way back at about a quarter to twelve. I'll be leaving even earlier. I have some work to do coordinating everything, you understand."

"Certainly, certainly. How long do you think we can expect you to stay?"

"I have to leave by eleven."

"That's fine. That gives us another, let me see, another forty minutes of your time. I'm sure Sheriff Gonzalo can make use of you for that time. If you'll both excuse me, I have some phone calls to make."

With that, he left the station house.

"So what are we off to do?" Susana asked.

"Well, I've got to start looking for deputies. It would be a big help if you could drive into the Valley, find my deputies, and begin knocking on doors. That's what we need the most right now."

"Where exactly are they in the Valley?"

"Well, I expect that Collazo, the older deputy, is probably out of his car just walking from house to house. Hector, the young one, will never be found more than a hundred feet from the squad car. Find the car, and you are bound to find the man."

Sheriff Ortiz was about to leave when she turned to Gonzalo as he was putting on his hat.

"Anything I should know about the people down in the Valley? Any suspicious characters to look out for?"

Gonzalo thought for a minute.

"No. They're just people. Martin Mendoza is one of the richest men in Puerto Rico. It might be hard to get onto his property if you get up to that property anyway. Leave him for one of my men. Other than that, there are no special characters down there. If you see anything suspicious, don't be afraid to investigate until you're satisfied."

With that, they left for their respective tasks.

CHAPTER NINE

It was nearly ten-thirty when Susana Ortiz arrived in the Valley and found Hector's squad car. Hector was somewhat harder to find.

The car was parked at the entrance to an unpaved off road branching off the main road. His car blocked the entrance, so Sheriff Ortiz pulled up behind it and followed the path over a small rise and into a clearing in what was otherwise thick forest. In the center of the clearing there was a small house, painted a sickly pea green. The house stood on stilts about two feet high, and instead of the white metal slat windows so common on the island, this house had wooden shutters and curtains only. Shutters and paint were original to the house, and it was clear that the house had been standing in the forest for half a century.

From where the house first became visible, Sheriff Ortiz could see Hector standing on the porch knocking on the door. As she drew closer, she heard him as he stuck his head in at a window.

"Come out!" he yelled. "It's not about you. I just need to talk to you."

He moved to the side of the house and stood on a metal pail to see in at a different window. Sheriff Ortiz ambled closer, watching him stick his head in at this window.

"Don Alonzo. I have no problem with you. I just need you to talk to me for one minute," he yelled into the house.

The shotgun blast tore through the wooden side of the house, taking off one of the shutters, blowing it into the bushes a few feet away. Wood splinters and bits of curtain cloth seemed to hang suspended in air for the half-second it took for Hector's body to arc to the ground with a thud, the half-second it took the metal pail beneath him to be kicked to a rest under the stilted house.

Sheriff Ortiz froze in her tracks ten yards from the deputy. Her next move was to pull her service revolver and run to Hector's side. He was moving when she got to him. While still flat on his back, he was trying to raise his hands to his face, but they were shaking wildly.

"Are you okay?" she yelled to him.

Hector looked at her with a look of utter disorientation that perfectly displayed the complete confusion he felt. He was positive he hadn't been shot, but how could he explain the beautiful woman cradling his head if he wasn't entering the Kingdom of Heaven? She repeated her question to him several times in quick succession, but, in fact, he heard nothing but a loud whistle and static combined.

The sheriff quickly assessed Hector and, finding no blood on his person, concentrated on the sound of the back door slamming shut.

Leaving Hector, she looked under the house to see a pair of legs wearing dress socks and slippers running away. With revolver in hand, she carefully turned the corner of the house just as Don Alonzo began to make his way into the woods.

"Don Alonzo!" she called, but he kept on into the woods.

Don Alonzo was not quite eighty years old and not quite five feet tall. He had on his slippers, his thick, dark-rimmed glasses, and a pair of plaid shorts pulled up high enough to cover most of his shirtless chest. Were it not for the double-barreled shotgun he carried and his obvious willingness to use it, he would have been a comical figure, especially as the weapon was no shorter than himself.

Sheriff Ortiz stayed a few yards behind Don Alonzo, not wanting to tackle a man with a shotgun, even if he looked like she could carry him in her back pocket.

They entered another clearing under several tall trees. In this spot, the sun had little chance to warm the ground so there was almost no undergrowth. There were, however, dozens of vines hanging off the tree limbs nearly to the ground. These were *bejucos picantes,* sharp-edged vines that would scratch through your skin, leaving hairs that could continue itching for a week if you didn't pick your path carefully through them. It was Don Alonzo's plan to rush through this area, losing the officer behind him in a sea of small pains. Since he had no shirt on and his hands were full, it soon became clear he was not going to be able to make his escape. He stopped a moment to think.

"Don Alonzo!" Susana yelled.

He turned, shotgun in hand, and the sheriff dropped to a knee and squinted at the hairs on his chest over the barrel of her gun.

"Drop your weapon, old man, or I'll kill you!"

Don Alonzo looked around himself, peering through thick

glasses. Evidently, they weren't thick enough because he seemed unable to find he source of the voice that was giving him commands.

"Drop the gun!" the sheriff repeated.

Don Alonzo dropped his gun, still looking for the source of the voice. Sheriff Ortiz bolstered her own gun, stepped on the shotgun, and handcuffed her prisoner.

"My shoulders itch," Don Alonzo said.

"What?" Sheriff Ortiz said in the meanest tone she could muster.

"What?" Don Alonzo replied.

"What did you say?"

"Who are you?" Alonzo asked.

Susana read him his Miranda rights before leaving the vine-infested clearing. She advised him repeatedly that he should remain silent as they walked back to the old man's house. Don Alonzo, however, wanted to talk. For the three minutes he walked ahead of her, he talked about the weather and what he planned to do to stay cool. He asked what time it was—he wanted to be positive he wasn't missing his favorite TV show, *El Show de las Doce.*

At Don Alonzo's house, Hector was sitting on the back steps, covering his ears with his palms and opening his mouth. He looked up when the shadows of the prisoner and sheriff fell upon him.

"You can let him go," he said too loudly.

"Let him go? Are you crazy, deputy? He tried to kill you. I don't care if he is old. He attempted to commit murder."

"It's not the first time. He's a little sick. He has Alzheimer's. He was robbed about four years ago. His children make sure he has a gun because he lives alone in the woods. They're afraid somebody'll hurt him."

"Somebody is going to hurt him if he keeps shooting at police officers. He's a menace to himself and others. I made the arrest, I say he takes a trip to town."

Hector opened his mouth and slapped at his ears.

"What?"

"I said I'm taking him in. I can't just overlook attempted murder of a police officer," she yelled.

"Okay, but it's a waste of time. One of his daughters is a judge. The first time he shot at me, I took him in. The judge for his case refused to listen to anything. Released him and reprimanded me for not understanding the elderly. The second time it happened, the judge ordered him to spend a week in a hospital because of his nerves; supposedly I scared him. Forget it; the day that old man kills me, he'll get a medal."

"Well, I'm still taking him in. They can reprimand me if they want. Anyway, how are you doing? You okay?"

"Look at my hands." Hector raised his hands. They were trembling fiercely.

"The first two times, he had handguns. I guess someone figured he had a better chance of hitting me with a shotgun. Son of a bitch unloaded both barrels on me. This is going to take me a few minutes to shake off."

"Well, if you weren't on duty, I'd tell you to drink a beer. I know you have to get back to searching for those children. I suggest you make tight fists, count to ten, and let go. Do this a few times, and your hands should go back to normal. Anyway, Deputy Pareda, I'm taking the old man in. I have deputies at the elementary school and the junior high school until 11:45. You and the other deputy, Collazo, should try to be there to see the kids leave, okay? Sheriff Gonzalo is collecting citizens to be deputized. Who knows? Maybe we'll put Don Alonzo here to work."

Sheriff Ortiz turned back to Don Alonzo, who had not stopped talking all this time.

"Wait a minute. How did you know my name?" Hector asked.

"Your nameplate's pinned to your chest."

Hector had seen the nameplate pinned to Sheriff Ortiz's chest, but he had avoided looking close enough to read it. He felt shy about searching her bosom for a name, especially when it had natural attractions of its own.

"What's your name?" he asked.

She smiled at him and stooped to present her nameplate for inspection. Though she hadn't planned it, in stooping she had presented the deputy with a clear sight of her cleavage; it was only by luck that he remembered to glance at the name on the nameplate as she pulled away.

"Ortiz. Sheriff of Naranjito?"

"That's me," she said.

She led her prisoner toward her car, and Hector paid close attention to her hips as she walked off. He paid attention to the length of her legs and to the ponytail of dark, wavy hair that he hadn't noticed before. He wanted to have some reason to call her back or some reason to follow her to the station house. When she had disappeared over the rise with Don Alonzo, Hector shuddered, and he found that his hands were finally still.

For his part, Emilio Collazo had a much easier time of his search. No one shot at him. Still, searching the houses in the Valley was difficult work. While many houses lined the main road, many others were hidden in the recesses of the surrounding woods. Many homes could only be approached by footpaths worn through grassy fields or dense underbrush. As Gonzalo had suspected, Collazo found it easier to park his car along the side of the road and walk from house to house.

When he heard the shotgun blast, he rushed to his car to radio Hector. Not getting a response, he drove down the road until he located the squad car. He met the sheriff of Naranjito getting into her car with the suspect when he pulled up.

"Who fired?" he asked.

Sheriff Ortiz pointed to Don Alonzo in the backseat.

"Again? Alonzo, *ya estás viejo*," Collazo called out. *You're old already.* "Stop shooting at people."

"I'm taking him to Naranjito; I know you guys are busy here. When all of this is over, have Gonzalo give me a call so we can talk about Don Alonzo here, okay?"

"Sure. Is the boy still in there?"

"Officer Pareda? Yeah, he's there. He's taking a minute to calm his nerves; otherwise he's fine."

"Good. I'll let you go about your business. Just remember—Don Alonzo is hard to handle if he doesn't watch his *Show de las Doce*, okay?"

"No problem. Oh, I should tell, you. You and Officer Pareda have to relieve my men at the elementary school and the junior high school at eleven forty-five. My deputies have to get back to Naranjito, you understand."

"Got it."

When Collazo came over the rise, Hector was stretching and trying to knock the dust off his back. After discussing briefly the incident with Don Alonzo, Hector had one question for Collazo.

"What did you think of her?"

"Who? The sheriff?"

"Who else?"

"I don't know. I only spoke to her for a minute," Collazo replied.

"Oh, come on. You're old, Collazo, not dead. Didn't you see her?" Hector asked unconsciously making a motion with his hands that outlined two large breasts.

Collazo laughed.

"Son, believe me when I say that, first of all, at my age it would take more than a minute for me to be attracted to a woman. Secondly, I would truly be a fool if I forgot, even for a minute, that I have a good wife at home. I was married before that girl's father was born."

"Okay, Collazo. I was wrong. You really are dead. Let's get back to work."

The two deputies walked back to their cars. It was eleven o'clock. Gonzalo found the deputies in the Valley separately a few minutes later. He brought six newly deputized citizens with him to help in the door-to-door work. He had mapped out a strategy for handling the school closing at noon. Since the work of going door to door was sometimes arduous and the new deputies needed to be supervised, Hector would stay working in the Valley. Collazo would be at the junior high school to make sure the kids got on the bus or left with some responsible adult. Gonzalo would go to the elementary school to do the same. Had everything worked according to plan, Angustias would have been spared much tragedy and pain. As it was, the day is remembered still for its griefs.

CHAPTER TEN

As the long-time principal of the elementary school (and sometimes acting head of the other schools), Agustin Martinez had been (still is) the mother hen of an entire generation-worth of Angustian childhood. He was passionate about *his* children to a degree many thought unhealthy for him, though imminently beneficial for his pupils. One morning, after seeing the children to their classrooms, he had locked himself into his office to agonize over a stabbing pain in his side. After much sweat, after silent tears, after breaking every pencil on his desk, and after seeing the kids back on the school bus in the afternoon, he had a teacher drive him to the hospital, where doctors removed an appendix ready to burst. No one bothered to ask him why he hadn't gone to the hospital earlier. Everyone knew his dedication to the children was complete. He would sacrifice himself for them as readily as he would sacrifice anyone else.

At one San Juan meeting, he had thrown a cup of coffee (contents and container) at the head of a politician who had dared to suggest that a cut in school funding would actually benefit the students; he had gotten himself into a physical confrontation with a parent he accused of child abuse; he was known to berate the mothers who berated their children. In all of this, Agustin Martinez had clearly stepped over professional and ethical boundaries, but for all of this, the parents of Angustias loved him, even if begrudgingly. After all, their children were the objects of his undivided efforts and attentions; nothing in his life came before them. Though he had gone through a series of relationships, he had never been able to find that perfect woman: the woman who could fully understand and accept that she would always come second in his life. His wife, in fact, had left him earlier that year. For such devotion, the parents of Angustias treated Agustin Martinez with a level of respect normally reserved for surgeons, judges, and self-made millionaires.

There was nothing out of the ordinary this day for the principal until the end of it. He had prowled in front of the school, waiting for the buses to arrive in the morning. This was his routine. It was too easy for a child to be struck by the cars that always passed by the school too fast for his liking no matter what their actual speed. It was also too easy for petty squabbles to turn into fistfights as the children milled about, waiting for class to begin. Lastly, it was too easy for the absent child to go unnoticed. For all these reasons, Martinez was out before the school bus arrived this day as every day.

In the neighborhood of the elementary school, there was nothing. No one lived nearby. There were fields on every side, but they were used for nothing. The nearest edifice of any kind was a candy store more than a thousand feet away. The school was like many in Puerto Rico. It had separate structures for each grade, along with a building for the bathrooms, one for the cafeteria, and one that served as Martinez's office. The buildings all sat on an open acre, and from the back of this acre, one could see across mountains and valleys and past the next town and the next.

Across the street from the school, there was a steep decline covered in dense underbrush. There was a metal highway guardrail that kept drivers from driving off the hill, and it was along this barrier that the children lined up after classes to await the bus. On this day, the children raced to the guardrail a few minutes before twelve o'clock. They quickly formed small groups—the boys playing marbles along the side of the road or crouching down to play at *gallito,* the girls playing ring games or variations on patty-cake. Some of the children of course, the older ones, gathered together, boy with girl, to carry on private conversations. Miguelina Roman formed one of these pairs. Her little brother watched the older boys play at marbles.

The bus pulled up alongside the guardrail at approximately five minutes after twelve. Behind it there was a red Toyota. The car was brand new, but did not draw any attention to itself. The children were all of them too busy forming a line to board the bus or finishing a game. When the car stopped behind the bus, this also did not garner notice. Several parents had already picked up their children and several students would be staying after the bus left, waiting for their parents to come for them. This obviously was just one of those parents or an uncle or a cousin.

The first person to notice the car and its driver was Miguelina. She was about to board the bus, talking with a friend, when she remembered to look for her younger brother Roberto. She spotted him as he closed the passenger-side door to the red Toyota he was in.

She froze in her place a moment, causing some slight frustration to the children behind her on line. As soon as the car moved out from behind the bus, she moved. Of course, she was far too slow to catch the car before it pulled out onto the road, but she didn't stop running. Miguelina headed straight for Martinez, who was crouched in serious conversation with a six-year-old about the state of her shoes.

"Mister, Mister! They took him! They took him!"

"Who? What?" Martinez asked.

"Roberto. Some man took Roberto. A gringo took Roberto," Miguelina said, pointing at the fast receding car.

Martinez squinted to make out the shape of the car. Had it not been that the car was a model heavily advertised on television, had it not been that, in fact, he wanted this exact type of car, he would not have been able to identify it. As it was, he no sooner identified it than he was racing to his own car. The red car disappeared over a rise, but in his last glimpse of the car's rear, Martinez noticed the turning signal was on.

One might think that a criminal could not be so stupid as to signal his intended route to everyone in sight, but seasoned criminals have done far stupider things, and the man driving the car was no seasoned criminal. He was, in fact, a nervous young man with a new bride waiting for him in a San Juan hotel. He had never driven a car away from the scene of a crime. He certainly had not thought that he should do anything differently on this drive than on any other drive. This lack of foresight caused him to signal to anyone who cared that he was turning left at the next intersection.

The fates that day were kind and cruel. Hector Pareda, in the squad car nobody but he cared to use, drove by the school not more than three or four seconds after Martinez was informed, fifteen or twenty seconds after the Toyota had driven off. Martinez was pulling out onto the street in his own car, ready to pursue the Toyota beyond the ends of the earth if needed. Seeing Hector, however, he cut him off with the back end of his car. He jumped out waving and screaming.

"Red Toyota! Some guy took Roberto Roman. Red Toyota! Go!"

"How long?" Hector shouted.

"Go! Left! Left!" Martinez replied, and Hector peeled away from the school.

Hector had asked "How long?" but he knew the answer was irrelevant. God would not have put him in just the right place, at just the right time, in just the right car, if a matter of seconds was going to be a factor.

Hector accelerated over the rise. The red Toyota ahead of him was doing no unusual speed. A curve in the road obscured Hector's view a moment, but the Toyota was soon again in sight, the driver apparently unaware that there was a squad car catching up to him. Hector floored the gas pedal. He would need to slow down for a moment where this road met the interstate. He would have to bring on the lights and sirens then. He hoped to be unshakably close by the time the interstate was reached.

He hoped also that one of the other officers would be joining the chase soon. Not that he needed help for the chase. This was one part of police work he excelled in, but the *Macheteros* were usually armed. They fought gun battles with the San Juan police, with the FBI, with ATF agents. They resisted arrest. They killed cops.

Hector shook off the thought and accelerated past the curve at eighty miles an hour. The interstate was a few hundred yards away, and the red car had already turned onto it. There was still no alarm in the fugitive's driving. Taking his foot off the gas pedal, Hector merged onto the interstate in one gigantic, unyielding curve.

Though his maneuver had technically done no harm, a pickup truck ran off the road more out of fear than because of any real danger. Hector didn't look back. Instead, he switched on the lights and sirens.

The interstate is a tourist panoramic-view road. It rolls gently along the tops of several hills and across several towns. At this point in the road, it sloped gently uphill for a mile or more before exiting Angustias. Hector wanted to stop the Toyota before entering any of the bordering towns. Not that his jurisdiction ended at the county line—all the police in Puerto Rico work for the state, reporting to their separate precincts but enforcing the same laws. But then, why would he want to share the arrest with someone who didn't have to answer to the parents of Angustias? Still, Hector wasn't unshakably close; the Toyota had already gone past an exit without making a move to lose the police car.

Hector wasn't unshakably close, but he was closing in. He was speeding at eighty miles an hour having zigged and zagged past all intervening traffic before the driver of the Toyota understood that the lights and the siren were for him. He accelerated past a second exit.

Hector flashed past a roadside fruit stand at nearly ninety miles an hour, and the young boy who had taken the half day off from school to tend to the business jumped into the underbrush from fear. Hector wasn't unshakably close, but he was gaining on the Toyota.

Inside the Toyota, the driver began to panic. He spent about as much time looking into the rearview mirror as he did watching the road. This was no sleepy sheriff coming after him. He knew he was approaching a hundred miles an hour, but the squad car was relentless in closing the gap. He was unaccustomed to these speeds, and he wasn't sure of the car's capabilities. He knew the third exit was coming up soon, and there was no way he could make the turn without decelerating sharply. He glanced at the little boy sitting quietly in the passenger seat. Roberto had stopped playing with the mutt puppy in his lap. He was instead staring out the window with curiosity. The driver thought for a moment of pulling over and giving up. But there was the exit coming up fast, and there was the squad car coming up fast.

He swerved toward the exit.

The moment the Toyota decided for the exit, Hector angled the squad car across the shoulder of the road, across the hard packed dirt beyond the shoulder. He traveled at a hundred miles an hour over ruts six inches deep. He hit his head against the car ceiling. The Toyota pulled away from the exit and continued on the interstate. Hector made a huge parabolic curve back onto the interstate, accelerating closer to the Toyota. As he flew past the exit, he saw the reason for the detour. Don José was leading his small herd of cows to a watering hole. The six of them took up the entire road, and they could neither be hurried nor plowed through.

High on that hill, parked on the third exit's road, was a blue Toyota. The driver of this car, a red-faced man nearing sixty, watched the missed entrance of both cars. He pulled out of his parking space and took a dirt road that joins with the road of the fourth exit. Because of a curve in the interstate, he would arrive on that road in time to develop whatever his plan was.

The fourth exit led to nothing. The driver of the red Toyota didn't know this and didn't care. All he cared was that this road might help him lose the squad car that was now much closer.

The incline was steeper on this new road. The road was narrow and, on this road, there was a metal guardrail, and all alongside the road there were sharp, disheartening drops. The driver knew there would be no forgiveness for any error. He thought again of stopping the car before the road killed him. The child beside him yelled out "Whoa" for each sharp turn and giggled. For Hector, the road following the fourth exit was familiar territory. He had once had a girlfriend who lived somewhere on these hills, and he had raced up and down these hills a hundred times, though rarely at this speed and never with this purpose.

He sped after his suspect at 105, then one 110, then one 115 miles an hour. He knew his car's limit. There was still an inch between the gas pedal and the car floor. He had once reached 140 miles an hour, but the car had stalled out on him before a minute at that speed had elapsed. Hector couldn't think of that now.

He knew his steering wheel was fighting him on every turn. He knew he was opening up on each curve far more than he liked. He knew that the coolant temperature gauge had begun climbing into the red zone. He knew that the car ahead of him was newer and that neither Gonzalo nor Collazo was anywhere in sight. He knew all these things and more. He knew also that the boy's life depended on his staying close, because at the back of his mind, always, there was a voice saying, "If you lose him, the boy dies." Over and over, the voice said this as he raced up the hill and around the curves. And the voice wasn't the helping voice of inspiration. Instead, it was a sniggering voice that taunted him as though urging him to give up, reminding him he wasn't good enough for this job.

With all these things in mind, can it be any wonder that Hector didn't see the blue Toyota waiting for him in the tall grass along the side of the road until it had already lurched out and clipped the back end of his car?

The driver in the blue Toyota had been aiming for the passenger side door. He wanted to send Hector and car off the hill altogether, but he hadn't calculated on the speed with which both cars would be passing him, and he had parked on grass which reduced his car's traction and hurt his ability to accelerate.

The hit to the rear of Hector's car did several things. First, it sheared the rear fender cleanly off the car, shooting it straight into the woods across the road. More importantly, it pitched the front end of the car into the metal guardrail that kept cars from going off the hill. This, even though Hector was fighting the steering wheel to stay on the road. The squad car scraped along this railing for several yards before Hector was able to pull the car back onto the road. This slowed him for a moment but no more than that. Most important of all, the collision with the blue Toyota broke a bolt in Hector's engine block. The metal piece shattered his oil filter, spilling the engine's lubricant. He wasn't sure at the time exactly what was happening, but he felt the car was about to give up on him. He heard a loud whizzing noise coming from under the hood. The red Toyota had widened the gap, and Hector heard the voice at some level in his thoughts reminding him that the boy would die if he lost the Toyota.

He floored the gas pedal. The sound from underneath the hood became a scream. The squad car began to fishtail. But the gap between the cars narrowed, then closed, and the instant the squad car stalled out and shut off, Hector rammed the red Toyota from behind.

Hector's car rolled to a halt as he watched the Toyota continue on, swerving from one side of the road to another and back again until finally the car flew off the hill. Hector sat frozen in horror a second, and a second later the blue Toyota sped past his car, stopping at the point where its companion had gone off the road. He tried starting the car. The driver of the blue Toyota stepped out of his car and looked down to where the other car had come to a stop. Then he made a U-turn, heading back toward Hector and his wreck.

There was little for Hector to do in trying to stop the blue Toyota. He tried putting the car in neutral, thinking to roll it downhill into the path of the oncoming car, but his car would have none of it. He settled for opening his door and stepping out, but before he could get a foot out, the blue Toyota slammed his car door shut as it passed by him. In that instant, as the second car drove past him, he looked at the driver with his mirrored sunglasses, his baseball cap, his disturbing red hair peeking out at the sides, and his luxuriously fat face. The features burned into his memory as he tried getting the license plate number through the rearview mirror. He got the first half—XI 9.

"Copy, copy, copy," he called into his CB.

"What is it, son?" Collazo answered.

"I need an ambulance at Sierra Las Puntas, kilometer three-point-nine."

"Is it the Toyota with the boy?" Collazo asked.

"Good. You heard about it," Hector said. "You're also looking for a blue Toyota Corolla, I think. Banged up in front. License begins with XI 9. What's your distance?"

"Two minutes. Gonzalo's coming too. He's farther out. You okay?"

"Can't talk. Got to see the kid. Get that ambulance. Pareda out."

With that, Hector tossed aside his CB and climbed out the passenger side after finding that his door wouldn't budge. He jogged the hundred yards to the point where the car had gone off the road.

It was found out by an FBI expert some time later that the Toyota could not have left the skid marks it did or flown as far as it did or hit the mango tree as high as it did, wouldn't have crumpled so completely or rebounded so forcefully, had it not left the road in excess of one hundred miles per hour.

CHAPTER ELEVEN

At 11:40 that morning, just as Gonzalo was heading to his post at the elementary school, Jorge Nuñez received a phone call from a man purporting to be speaking for *Los Macheteros*. The man was long-winded and angry, signs that his call was more a hoax than an actual threat, but Jorge Nuñez was not at all aware that terrorist threats are always short and often businesslike. Instead of shrewdly evaluating the message, weighing each word to judge its worth, Jorge scribbled every word he could onto his desk blotter.

While the caller raved for a full five minutes or more, the deputy mayor boiled the message down to a few harsh words: "We took young children in Aibonito; we're going to take older ones from you." For some reason, this seemed like a logical proposition to Jorge. A second part of the message was translated as, "We're going to fight your police force; we'll attack at the weakest link."

Now, much more than this had been said, some of it in direct conflict with what Jorge Nuñez copied over on a small piece of paper. But, like a fortuneteller who may find anything they desire in the leaves at the bottom of a bowl of tea, Jorge found his greatest fears in the scribblings on his blotter. Though other phrases on the blotter might have given him hope of Angustias being spared altogether, what he found important and what he related to Gonzalo over the CB, was terrible.

"*Los Macheteros* called," he told Gonzalo. "They're going to attack the junior high school. They're going to go after Collazo."

No rational person would have put the same construction on the words on Jorge's blotter; his interpretation was based more on fear than on what he had actually written down. He had a child in the junior high school; he didn't trust Collazo's ability to watch an entire school by himself. He had visions of the seventy-two-year-old deputy asleep under a tree while all the children were taken off by a terrorist in a black ski mask.

Jorge Nuñez's interpretation was false, but there was no way Gonzalo could know that. The message he was given was transparently clear. Gonzalo raced for the junior high school, driving past the elementary school, calling Hector on the CB.

"Get to the elementary school. *Los Macheteros* called. They're going to the junior high school. I'm going to reinforce Collazo."

Hector said he understood the instructions and put the CB down on the passenger seat and stepped on the gas pedal again, trying to free his car from a small patch of slick mud and wet grass. It occurred to him to inform Gonzalo of his situation, but he quickly rejected the idea. Gonzalo could do nothing to help him; he had a mission of his own to accomplish.

When he finally managed to get free of the mud, he raced to the elementary school, hoping to position his car in front of the school bus. He planned to check the occupants and the driver to make sure everyone on the bus belonged there. Principal Martinez stopped him before he got to the bus. The happenings of the next eight minutes—the chase and crash—are known.

The descent to the crushed Toyota was a steep one, so steep Hector soon decided against making it. He tried walking his way down but slipped on the second step; only a fistful of grass kept him from sliding to the bottom of the hill. He thought of the stretch of utility rope in the trunk of his car, but the picture of him trying to make the right knot came with the idea, so he opted for a third route to the wreck. Farther up the hill, there was a gentler slope to a point below the car; from there, he could work his way up.

He worked his way downhill then uphill again, and for the two or three minutes he spent in the woods pushing aside branches and tall grass, he imagined a profound silence. He heard his own breathing and his footsteps, and he wondered whether the driver was still alive. He felt as though there was an eye watching him from above, judging him, and he wanted someone to blame for what was turning into an embarrassingly bad day.

From a distance, he saw Collazo already at the car, looking into the passenger-side window.

"How'd you get here?" he yelled out from twenty feet below the crash site.

Collazo looked down at him with pain scrawled onto his face.

"Stay where you are, son."

"What do you mean?" Hector asked, climbing slowly. "I'm all right. I can help."

"These two don't need help. Stay where you are."

"Is that an order?" Hector asked.

"Yup."

In actuality, Collazo had no authority to order his junior colleague to do anything, but his gray hair had earned Hector's respect, so the younger man stayed where he was at a point a dozen feet below the car. From there, his view was limited by a banana tree and several large-leafed *malanga* plants. He could see only part of the driver's side of the car, but no driver was visible, and part of the smashed front of the car was visible. The vehicle itself rested at an angle against the mango tree that had stopped its flight off the hill. The two front tires dangled a foot off the ground. He could also see that a bite had been taken out of the tree. When he looked closely at his surroundings, he found a dozen large splinters, one the size of a baseball bat.

It was when Collazo moved to the driver's side of the car, nearer to Hector, that he was able to make out what he had been hearing as the older deputy's mumbling. Collazo had begun a prayer for the dead.

Collazo ducked his head in the driver's-side window, and Hector could hear him ask, "Do you want a priest? Would you like to confess your sins?"

Gonzalo called out to Collazo from the road above the wreck. "How is it down there?"

"Is the ambulance coming?" Collazo responded.

"Yeah. Twenty minutes. The doctor will be here in two."

Gonzalo took a cautious step over the twisted metal divider, and

Collazo pointed out a zigzag path to the car. Gonzalo moved from tree to stump to dense clump of grass to tree to the car, jogging between each point to go with gravity's flow rather than against it. He made his way to the driver's side.

"How's he doing?" he asked before peeking into the car for himself.

"Not too good. In and out. I asked him if he wanted a priest. No answer."

"And the kid?"

"Dead."

"Damn. You sure?"

"Believe me."

Gonzalo moved to the passenger side of the car. With only a second or two of examination, his knees weakened, and he fell sitting on the forest floor. Hector could hear the deep moaning coughs of a man trying to hold back tears. This was the only sound in the forest, and Hector understood then that he had been spared an image that would have haunted him unceasingly.

"Collazo. You go back into town. Get six more men, no, ten. I want every child in this town accounted for ASAP. Then get back here. I don't know how we're going to get this car out of here, but we are. Hector, take my car." Gonzalo tossed his keys to Collazo, who relayed them to the deputy below. "We need to start looking for that second Toyota. If we can catch him, we can find Samuel and Lydia. Get on your CB; tell everyone what we're looking for. We consider this man armed and dangerous until we find out different. Let's move, guys. There's lots to do."

Hector pocketed the keys and climbed the hill on all fours, hanging onto roots and vines to pull himself up. Collazo stayed behind a little.

"What are you going to do?" he asked Gonzalo.

"Me? I've got to stay here until the doctor gets here; I have to search this car. I've got plenty to do. Get moving, Collazo. Don't worry about me."

Collazo left, climbing the hill in the same way Hector had done before him, but he could not easily stop worrying. He thought of both the younger officers as sons, though he refrained from calling Gonzalo that in public. Knowing Gonzalo's temperament, Collazo was aware that the sheriff would take this case personally, that the sight of the boy's broken body would have some effect on Gonzalo's soul. He knew that his oldest "son" was impressionable and would suffer over this case for weeks to come.

In the minute or two between Collazo's departure and the doctor's arrival, Gonzalo took a closer look at the occupants of the car.

Roberto Roman was dead; there was no doubt of this. He had not been strapped in with a seat belt. When the car left the road, his body had left the seat. He'd hit the car's ceiling and plopped back into his seat in the instant before impact with the mango tree. Roberto had crashed into the windshield shoulder first; the inertial forces had snapped his head into the glass, breaking his skull and the neck it rested on. Where his skull had fractured, there was an indentation as though someone had sliced away a piece. Gonzalo studied the boy's deflated head a moment. He recalled that just a day or two earlier, he had seen Roberto smiling and laughing. His eyes had sparkled and his laughter had come out in short bursts of high-pitched giggles. Gonzalo caught himself thinking of the dim eyes that would never open again and of the crushed throat that would make no more sounds.

"This isn't useful," he told himself, but the subject was irresistible.

"What do I say to the Romans?" he wondered. " 'Roberto died

quickly and at an age when his innocence ensured a peaceful end.' What will words like these mean to them?" he thought to himself.

There was a movement on the driver's side. Gonzalo rushed to the driver, who was whispering something.

The driver was folded over with the seat belt across his chest keeping his head from touching the steering wheel.

"What'd you say?" Gonzalo asked.

The man mumbled something incomprehensible.

"You guys make me sick, you know that? You want independence? Fine, maybe that's not a bad idea, but look at what you did. You murdered the boy, murdered him. And for what? For nothing. Terrorism is a federal case. They're gonna strap you into the chair, and if there's any justice in this world, they'll give me the honor, the joy of flipping the switch on you and ending your stupid life."

All of this Gonzalo hissed out between clenched teeth. As he spoke and worked out the driver's crimes in his mind—terrorism, treason, kidnapping, and murder, crimes against the country and the city of Angustias, against God and the Romans—Gonzalo grew more enraged with his motionless suspect. The thought flashed in his mind that if the suspect would only resist, try to escape, he could empty out his gun and give vent to the fury inside himself.

The man, of course, understood few of the words directed at him, but all the sentiments were plainly carved into the lines of Gonzalo's face. The driver wouldn't turn his head to face the sheriff. He knew he had broken his neck. He couldn't move his toes or his legs. He couldn't move his arms, though he could wiggle his fingers and make weak fists. He felt that any movement might kill him, but he wasn't sure he wouldn't welcome death if only it would come quickly.

"So what do you have to say for yourself? Don't you have some kind of speech ready? Wasn't this part of your master plan?" Gonzalo taunted.

The man had no reply for Gonzalo, though he could tell from the tone of his voice that an answer of some kind was expected. He couldn't think of anything to say that would change the circumstances he had put himself in. He looked at Gonzalo through the corner of his eye. From this angle, his view of the sheriff was distorted; he appeared large and unhuman.

"I'm sorry," he whispered.

Gonzalo stood mute with tremors of rage running through his body. Of all the things the suspect could have said, "I'm sorry" was possibly the worst. It sounded to Gonzalo like mockery. That the man spoke English suggested nothing more to Gonzalo than that he had just wasted his efforts in talking to the man. Though Gonzalo was completely fluent in English, he felt then that there was no possibility of making himself understood to the limp thing before him.

"I'm sorry," the man repeated.

Gonzalo felt dizzy. He could sense the juices in his stomach roiling. His mind went white with despising. He ducked his head in through the driver's window, whispering an inch away from the man's ear.

"Your neck broke?"

"I think so," the man whispered. "Maybe not all the way . . ."

Before the man could say, "I can still move my fingers," Gonzalo had seized him by the hair and jammed his head back onto the headrest. A loud snap came from the man's neck. The sound startled Gonzalo, but that didn't make him stop forcing the man's head back. The sound of the doctor's voice calling to him from the road above made him stop.

"Gonzalo! Don't do anything for him! I'll be down in a minute," the doctor said, and, being a young man still, he jumped over the metal barrier. Without having ever gained a firm foothold, the doctor slid downhill flat on his back as though he were a luge-team member. Gonzalo had to take two careful steps to the side to position himself to stop the doctor's ride. The activity of helping the doctor to his feet allowed Gonzalo to escape close inspection. He was blushing. With the doctor there and time to think, Gonzalo realized that he had come close to murdering the invalid. As it was, he had probably worsened the man's condition. He wondered how many arrests he had made over the years for actions far less rash, far less violent, and with fewer consequences than what he had himself just done. As he helped the doctor to the driver's side, Gonzalo wondered what he would have done had he killed the man.

Doctor Perez peered in at the driver and began asking questions Gonzalo couldn't hear and performing tests Gonzalo couldn't see. After a minute or less, he stood upright and turned to the sheriff.

"This man's got a broken neck. There's some swelling that will shut off his ability to breathe in a few minutes. However, he's refusing medical treatment and . . ."

"He doesn't have that option, Doctor. You're going to do everything you need to do to keep him alive."

"I can't just treat a patient against his wishes, Gonzalo. If he were unconscious, that would be one thing, but he's lucid. . . ."

"That man is a *Machetero*."

"So what?"

"He knows where the two missing kids are. Either he's going to tell us or we're going to trade him to *Los Macheteros* for the kids. In any event, he's no good to us dead."

"I still can't just . . ."

"Doctor, if you let this man die, you'll be letting Samuel Villareal and Lydia Femandez die. Do you see why that is not going to happen?" Gonzalo asked, taking a step closer to the physician.

Dr. Perez thought about the options for a moment, biting at his thumbnail. Ever since coming to Angustias, he had found dealing with the sheriff difficult. He knew Gonzalo was an intelligent man, but he could never seem to understand that suspects couldn't always be wakened and interrogated or released to a jail cell or courtroom. Witnesses were not always in a condition to talk; patients had rights. These also were concepts that Gonzalo did not like to admit. Still, Perez saw the urgency in this case, and he never liked to let a patient die while he waited around to note the time.

"Okay. Tell the tow-truck guy to throw down the bag I brought with me. We can intubate the patient here. We can squeeze air into his lungs by hand, but we need to get him to the clinic. We have a hand-me-down respirator. If it works, fine; if not, we have to get him to Ponce, okay?"

"Sure."

"We also need a flat board or something so we can get him out of here."

Gonzalo called for Luis Velez, the tow-truck operator. Luis happened to be carrying two lengths of two-by-twelve, which he used to put under the wheels of cars stuck in the mud. In a matter of minutes, both the driver of the Toyota and Roberto Roman, the passenger, had been pulled up from the wreck by the winch on the tow truck. Both bodies were laid on the back of the truck, the doctor riding with them to insure the patient's air supply. Gonzalo stayed with the car, searching it.

The trunk lock had been forced open by the force of the crash, so he started there. There was nothing peculiar in the trunk, though everything was in disarray. The spare and jack, the plastic jug of coolant, the empty two-gallon gas can, and a funnel were all there, all new. There was a blanket that didn't seem to have come with the car, but there was nothing special about it. The car was clearly a rental, and the papers for it were probably in the glove compartment. That is where Gonzalo checked next.

The glove compartment contained the usual owner's manual, road map of Puerto Rico, and the rental papers from Hertz that showed the driver's name as Julio Acevedo. Gonzalo thought for a second on the possibility that the name was a phony but returned to his search before making any decision. The next item he found was a five-by-eight manila envelope. Gonzalo spilled the contents onto the passenger seat. There was a set of two small keys of the type used with padlocks. There was a scrap of paper with three names: Julio Acevedo was separated from the other two by a double line. Jonathan Chetham and David Poole; neither name was familiar.

The third item in the envelope was a pornographic picture of an older man, not the driver, with a young boy, not from Angustias, naked on a sofa. Though Gonzalo had on his driving gloves, he dropped the photo as though it had burned him. He had never imagined anything as vile as what he had just let go. He took a step back from the car. The image burned itself into his mind every time he closed his eyes. He jammed his palms into his eyes, scrunching them closed, hoping to blank the picture out of his mind, but it recurred. Gonzalo vomited out the little bit of toast and coffee he still had in his stomach. He kept retching long after there was anything left in him. The image wouldn't go away. It was two full minutes before Gonzalo could force himself to continue the search of the car.

There was nothing else in the glove compartment, but the driver's seat had a small pile of change and a hotel room key from the

San Juan Hilton. These had slipped out of the driver's pockets.

"Gonzalo!" Hector called for him from the road at the top of the hill. "Gonzalo. They have the second driver. He's in custody."

Gonzalo collected his evidence, the keys, the photo, the list of names, the information on the car. He folded the photo twice to keep it from exposing itself again. He was about to leave the wreck, when he heard a puppy's whimper. The little mutt had been thrown to the backseat, unharmed. Gonzalo took the dog in one hand and scampered up the hill for the ride back into town.

"Where to, chief?"

"The clinic. I need to get what I can from the first guy before I confront the second. The clear case is against the guy we pulled out of the wreck. Maybe he'll give us something against the other guy."

Gonzalo smiled weakly at his deputy. He enjoyed sharing his thoughts with Hector. He thought of the younger man as the next sheriff of Angustias and was careful to pass on any crime-fighting wisdom he had gained intact.

Hector drove quickly and said little during the short drive. This was appropriate, given the situation, but it didn't give him the time to apologize for the death he knew he had caused.

CHAPTER TWELVE

In fact, it had not been very difficult to catch the man in the second Toyota. He drove straight to a gas station in Comerio, and a deputy there put a gun to his head as he was tipping the man who had just filled his gas tank. His plan had been to get the gas, retrieve his things from the hilltop shacks, and head for anyplace far from Angustias, leaving his colleague and the little boy behind.

Hector's description—red hair, red face with mirrored sunglasses—could not have fit any other person in any of the towns surrounding Angustias. With the gun metal pressed to the back of his head, the man raised his hands and said calmly, *"No hablo español."* The red-haired man, David Poole as it turned out, had simply never considered that he might be caught by the Puerto Rican police force, a police force he had outwitted several times over the past three decades. He went along quietly. This arrest was merely a disagreeable but not overwhelming disturbance to his plans. A phone call would bring a lawyer who would clear up everything. As the officers guided him onto the backseat of their cruiser, he calculated he would be free by next sunup if not earlier.

Unlike the station house in Angustias, the one in Comerio was a new structure. It had half a dozen desks and room for more, and there were several computers throughout the office. There were six holding cells and two interrogation rooms, and while the gun rack in the Angustias station house held pump-action shotguns, the gun rack in Comerio had a half-dozen automatic weapons to complement the shotguns.

The red-haired man received his first hint that things might not go as smoothly as he hoped when the squad car pulled up in front of the station house. There were two officers in riot gear cradling automatic rifles waiting by the door of the precinct. Inside, there were two other officers in riot gear with shotguns. A third officer, Sheriff Molina, was trying to strap his torso into a blue bulletproof jacket.

"¡Caramba!" he yelled, giving up on the fantasy that he could ever make the front and back of his armor meet at his sides.

David Poole smiled weakly at the sheriff. Molina was nearly his age, and David certainly knew the troubles of trying to fit into clothes that refused to cooperate. Molina, a violent man always, saw the suspect's smile and did not appreciate it. He was flustered and in no mood to be mocked even by a *Machetero* who might have accomplices driving to his rescue or a bomb hidden on his person. He picked his .45 off the desk in front of him and made his way to the suspect. He put the gun barrel to David Poole's forehead.

"Ven conmigo y sin molestar, porque te meto una bala por enseguida."

Poole had lied earlier when he said he spoke no Spanish; he had learned the language years earlier when he first entered the business of supplying young boys to wealthy men, but Molina had shot out his words at a pace only a native would be able to understand. When Molina turned and began leading the way, Poole had no idea he had been told to follow him without causing trouble. The two officers behind him each shoved him forward. When Poole turned to confront the officers—he thought it wise to confront them before they began taking more serious liberties—Molina grabbed him by his manacled hands and tugged him to the rear of the station house. The more serious liberties had begun.

Molina dragged Poole into a cell and backed him up against the front of the small room. He shot out orders in Spanish that Poole couldn't pick up, and a deputy used a second pair of cuffs to secure him to the bars.

Poole began his protests.

"I'm an American citizen. I don't speak Spanish. I want to make my phone call."

Molina looked at him with some anger.

"¿Crees que yo sea pendejo?" he asked. Do you think I'm an idiot?

An officer with a shotgun was left to watch Poole, and he began to think his encounter with the law might not go so well. Still, he was sure they could not match his intellect. It would be uncomfortable, but he would be patient.

In the Angustias clinic, Irma Pagan, the only nurse on call at that hour, replaced Dr. Perez in regulating the patient's breathing. Luis Velez, the tow-truck operator, was asked to help get the respirator running. Without adjustment, it refused to work for more than a few minutes at a time.

"But I have to get back to work. I've got kids to feed," he complained.

"We'll pay you," the doctor answered. "How much do you make per hour?"

"When I have work, you mean?"

"Of course when you have work. How much do you charge? Don't worry, the city will pay it. We need this man to survive."

This proposition presented Luis with a singular opportunity—though he owned the only tow truck in town, most people preferred to have him take their cars to Domingo Ramos, the only other mechanic in town. Truth be told (and why not tell it?), most people preferred to push their cars to Ramos's shop rather than deal with Velez at all. He wasn't a good mechanic, he smelled, and he always had a sad story about why he was unable to complete work but needed to be paid anyway.

"I get twenty-five dollars an hour," he lied.

"Fine. We'll pay. Just sit here and make sure that machine runs, okay?"

The doctor walked out to the hallway. He knew nothing about Velez's usual rate of pay (never more than ten dollars an hour) or his mediocre skills as a mechanic. He only knew that his patient was in stable though critical condition and that Velez had a strange smell. Unless there was an emergency, there was no reason for him to remain near the odor.

Gonzalo hurried into the clinic. In his mind, hesitating at all before confronting the other suspect in Comerio was a calculated risk. He wanted to conduct his interview as quickly as possible.

"How's he doing?" he asked the doctor.

"Well, he'll never walk again. He won't be speaking anytime soon. If the swelling goes down in the next few hours, there is some possibility he'll have enough surviving nerve tissue to be able to breathe on his own, but I doubt it. Otherwise, he'll have the tube down his throat forever."

"Can he understand me if I talk to him?"

"Well, he's a bit groggy right now, but there's no reason why he can't, especially once he's rested a little. I guess you want to talk to him now, right?"

Gonzalo said nothing. He walked into the patient's room and out again.

"What's Luis Velez doing in there?"

"The respirator needs to have a mechanic around in case it breaks down."

"Velez was the best you could get?"

"He was here. He's fixed it twice in twenty minutes. That's good enough for me. When the patient has rested a bit, we'll need to get him to Ponce; they have a—"

"When I'm done with the patient, you can take him off the respirator."

"I can't do that. Even a *Machetero* has rights."

"He's not a *Machetero.*"

"Then what is he?" the doctor asked.

"Believe me, doctor, I have no explanation for what he is. He's not from the same world as you and I."

Gonzalo gave the doctor what he hoped was a meaningful stare, but it was undecipherable to the doctor.

The sheriff went back into the room and ordered Velez out. He closed the door and walked slowly to the patient's bedside and leaned over the metal railing. He looked into the patient's eyes, and they looked back at him.

"I know you're in there, but I honestly don't know what you are," Gonzalo said.

The man looked away. Gonzalo stared at him a minute longer. Most crimes have an easily reducible motive: greed, anger, hatred, lust. Gonzalo had felt all these emotions to at least some degree. Understanding criminals was rarely very difficult. But this was different. Could the man in front of him have desired a little boy he didn't even know in that way? The idea seemed so foreign, though he had dealt with this type of crime before.

In his first summer as sheriff, a mother had come to him in the morning, screaming. Her baby, a three-year-old girl, was missing. Often, the fact that a child has gone missing for an hour or two means nothing. This was not one of those times.

The sun rose to its full height; the heat rising off the asphalt of the roads, making waves in the air, was the only breeze. The child had been playing in the shade in front of the house in a poor district of Angustias while the mother tended clothes on a line at the back of the house. The girl would not have been alone more than half an hour, but the mother had searched for her for two hours before walking a mile to the station house—her husband had the car at work in another city and she had no phone. She was distraught.

Knowing her point of origin, knowing how slowly a child her size would walk, knowing that some areas had already been searched by the mother, Gonzalo still had more area to cover than he could manage alone. And the sun was against him. The child could have gotten sick or fallen; she could have fainted from the heat and thirst. Or, Gonzalo thought to himself but did not say out loud, someone could have driven that lonely road and seen the girl, put her quickly in the car, and gotten to anyplace on the island by the time he first heard of the disappearance. He called on the mayor, the priest of the parish, and several discreet citizens to help canvas the woods, the farms, the streams, and the lake; they searched the abandoned houses, sheds, and animal pens. As the sun began to lower, he called on more citizens, and he called on the precincts adjoining Angustias. Sheriff Molina of Comerio asked if he had considered abduction. Gonzalo lied and said, "It doesn't look like that's what happened."

As the air began to cool and twilight approached, Gonzalo found the girl. She was in an open field overgrown with grasses eight miles from where she had started near the north border of the town. Someone had taken her from her home in a car and left her in the wild, two yards from the road. There were tire tracks where the grass was matted, there were two cigarette butts, and there was her naked, bleeding body. She had been raped, she had been sodomized, and she had been left to die. His heart did not beat the second he saw her; he felt terrible cold, his hands shook violently, and the muscles of his chest and back tightened painfully. The knot that formed in his throat felt large enough to kill him. He swallowed to dislodge it, his heart started again, and he tore his shirt off despite his chills, unable to struggle with the buttons. He wrapped the girl, carried her to the squad car, placed her on the wide seat next to him and drove to the only clinic in the area; at the time, it was in the next town. He steered with one hand, held her with the other, and willed her to live all the way.

At the clinic, the doctors separated him from her, and he paced, furious, in a tight elliptical path. It took only a few minutes for a doctor to come to him and say, "There is nothing we can do. She has bled too much, and she continues to bleed."

Gonzalo stayed with the girl, holding her as she lay on the examining table. He wanted to ask her questions as her life ebbed from her—anything that would help him find her killer—but he didn't. Her eyes were opened in his direction, but he could tell they didn't see him. They were like black marbles, useless and cold. She died in his arms.

He sometimes thought that child molesters must be very sick people who were in need of care along with their punishment. He could not feel that much pity for the man on the bed.

Gonzalo took out his handcuffs and positioned the patient's arm so that it lay along the bed railing.

"I want you to know," he said, cuffing the man to the bed. "I want you to understand that you will never live another day as a free man. I want you to realize that you will never walk again. You will never talk again. If you live another fifty years—and I hope you live at least fifty years—if you live to be a hundred years old, you will be chained to a bed every minute of every day. If you are hungry, someone will have to feed you. If you wet your sheets, somebody else will have to clean up. You understand what I'm telling you? From now until you die, if your nose itches, no one will know, no one will care, and no one will scratch. You have made your own special purgatory. You understand me?"

Gonzalo said all of this into the man's face, speaking in a fierce whisper. There were tears making their way to the man's pillow, but even then Gonzalo, usually a very sensitive man, felt only unmitigated hostility.

"Good. Now I need some answers from you."

Gonzalo brought forth the evidence he had collected at the crash site and laid them on the suspect's chest. He held up the photo so the suspect could see it.

"Do you know this man? Blink once for yes, twice for no."

The suspect blinked once.

"Was this man in a blue Toyota earlier today? Once for yes, twice for no."

The man blinked once.

"Is he Jonathan Chetham?"

Two blinks.

"David Poole?"

One blink.

A series of questions helped the sheriff understand a great deal of what the suspect had intended by abducting Roberto Roman, but he could get nowhere on the whereabouts of the other two children. Gonzalo imagined they had been smuggled out of Puerto Rico or were dead.

"Look. There's no reason to hold out on me. You will never see those kids. David Poole will never see them either. Just tell me where they are, okay?"

Two blinks. Gonzalo's small store of patience was used up.

"Look. If those kids die because you refuse to talk to me, I will make your life worse than you can imagine. Tell me what I need, and I won't put ashes in your eyes."

Gonzalo tried to think of the crudest things to say to the young man in front of him; he wanted to force cooperation, but everything he could think to threaten seemed stupid to him, petty and small.

"Come on, Anthony." Anthony Borden had committed his crime while carrying a wallet full of I.D.s. "What do you think? Do you think it will go easier on you if we don't find the kids? Believe me. For what you did today, there isn't a jury in P.R. that will give you less than life in a prison hospital. That's without showing this piece of filth you were carrying around. We're gonna save that picture for the trial of Mr. Poole. Poole is in a cell in Comerio, and I guarantee you, if you won't talk to us, Sheriff Molina will make Poole sing like a bird. He'll tell us all about how you masterminded the whole thing. You understand me? I need to know where Lydia Fernandez and Samuel Villareal are now. I don't care which of you tells me. Are you going to help me find them?"

Anthony blinked twice, and Gonzalo walked out of the room. What the sheriff had seen as the prisoner's recalcitrance was actually a combination of tiredness, confusion, and a desire to be honest. When the question about the other two children was put to him in its clearest form, he answered "no" because it was the literal truth. He would not be helping Gonzalo find the children because he had never seen them before. He wanted to let Gonzalo know that he had nothing to do with the disappearance of Samuel and Lydia, knew nothing about them at all, but in his dazed and weary state, confined to a vocabulary of "yes" or "no," he couldn't think of a way to convey this information.

Gonzalo found Hector in the hallway.

"I've got a job for you. Get to San Juan as fast as you can go in my car. Call ahead for backup to meet you at the San Juan Hilton, Room 302. Here's the key. I'll have Nuñez call for a warrant. Search the room; bring back any evidence."

"Evidence of what?"

"You're looking for plane tickets, passports, large sums of money, traveler's checks, anything that might suggest a conspiracy to kidnap children, transport them out of Puerto Rico, sell them. Fake I.D.s, disguises, whatever. Find out if our friend was seen with anyone. If he checked in with someone, arrest them. You're looking for two accomplices—Jonathan Chetham and Julio Acevedo. Probably aliases. Got it?"

"What do I charge them with?"

"For now? Conspiracy to kidnap, kidnapping, murder, charge them with whatever you want. Don't charge them at all, just bring them here. I need to talk to them. Any questions?"

"Yeah, just one. Is that *americano* a *Machetero?*"

"Anthony Borden? No. He's not a *Machetero*. I can understand one of those. Anthony is a pedophile."

"A what?"

"A pedophile."

"What's that?"

Gonzalo paused a moment not knowing how to satisfy curiosity without giving detail.

"A pedophile is a . . . a monster," he said.

Hector could make it to the center of San Juan in twenty minutes with lights and sirens on. He had done it before. But Gonzalo's car was not the color of a squad car; people might hear the siren but not know where it was coming from. If they didn't clear a path for him, it would take slightly longer. He told Gonzalo he would be at Room 302 in thirty minutes. Twenty-six minutes later, he met with four officers of the metropolitan police force in the lobby of the San Juan Hilton.

The metropolitan police are somewhat different from the state police of Puerto Rico. They wear blue instead of green; they patrol large cites, not hill towns; they have different weapons though the same pay, and they sometimes get more respect from the public than the officers who patrol the "cane fields and cow pastures." The officers themselves rarely share this prejudice, but when these officers saw that they had been waiting for Hector, they groaned out loud. It wasn't just that he was wearing a green uniform—he was also twenty-two years old, and the other officers were each old enough to be his father.

"Hey, boy, you here to shine shoes?" was the first question asked of him.

"What? Can't reach your own feet? Go on a diet, you slob. When you can see your toes again, maybe you'll find other parts you haven't seen in a while. . . . Unless it fell off."

The officer who had started the war of wits lost his toothy grin, but the other three thought the banter was hilarious.

"I'm here to search room 302. You're here to provide assistance. Two of you should ask at the front desk if they know anything about the guest in 302. Especially if they've been seen with anyone—a man or child, anyone. Ask the bellboys, the cleaning crew, the bartender . . ."

The metropolitan police smiled in amusement. One said something about a "child" pretending to give orders; another compared Hector to a department-store guard. Hector continued in an even voice:

"The man we have in Angustias killed a six-year-old boy this morning. He has raped several other boys. He was kidnapping children to sell them off the island. We think Room 302 is his home base. You guys don't want to work? Fine. He has friends on the island. I hope they don't take your kid next."

Hector stormed off and two serious-faced officers followed him up the stairs. The other two started their investigations on the ground floor after one of them had called in for two more uniformed police to help in the canvassing.

A clerk from the metropolitan courthouse was waiting in front of the room door when Hector arrived. He had a warrant in hand and handed it to Hector, leaving without a word.

The hotel staff recalled the people in 302. No children had been seen, though there was a woman, a newlywed bride.

Inside the room, there was little of note: money, but not a huge sum; plane tickets, but to no exotic locale—Miami. There were no passports, no fake I.D.s, no disguises, no children. There was a good quantity of women's clothing; twenty minutes into the search, a woman arrived.

"What's going on?" she asked.

"Do you know Anthony Borden?" Hector responded.

"We're married," Mrs. Borden said, and Hector put her in hand-cuffs, put her in his car, and drove to Angustias.

CHAPTER THIRTEEN

A minute after Hector drove out of Angustias, Jorge Nuñez received a call from the FBI. They had gotten lost driving through the hills of Puerto Rico, and they wouldn't be coming over anytime soon. The two children from Aibonito had been found, one dead, one alive. The girl had been stabbed. The boy had been forced to watch the execution by the *Macheteros,* and they had dumped him along with the girl's body in a cow pasture. A long diatribe pinned to the boy's shirt blamed the United States for causing the girl's death—the extreme action was necessary (sadly unavoidable) because of the American presence in Puerto Rico. They minimized the enormity her murder represented—she was better off dead than under the yoke of American oppression, etc.

This hopelessly artificial message carried in it one patently false detail. The *Macheteros* had claimed to have waited for an American response until they could wait no longer, that is, until noon. But the boy, once he had been given a muscle relaxant to calm his shuddering, asserted that she had been killed in the night. This assertion, confirmed by forensics at the scene, meant the girl had been murdered before anyone but her parents had known she was missing.

Of course, the deputy mayor could only imagine the worst for the missing children of Angustias. So far, only a hurried phone call from Gonzalo hinted that the abductor had not been a *Machetero*. The information that the *Macheteros* had visited the area outweighed the possibility that they had missed his town. Still, there was a glimmer of hope in the news from Aibonito. First of all, only one of the two children had been killed. To a man who was growing more desperate with each minute, this was good news. Secondly, the children had been found in Aibonito. The *Macheteros* had taken the children to an abandoned field only a few miles from their homes. With any luck, Nuñez thought, Samuel and Lydia were still in Angustias. They would be found through the house-to-house search, he told himself. As it turned out, he was right.

Raul Ruiz found Lydia on the land behind his store. Ruiz's property was rugged and uphill. Though he had been asked to search it earlier in the day, he waited for a second request before he thought of closing his store for an hour to conduct the search. He was getting old for this type of work, he complained. What he meant was that since his left hand had been shot off in a robbery attempt the year before, he had not felt the same in any aspect. In fact, some thought he might have lost his mind—he continued to change the dressing on his stump though the wound had healed months before.

Ruiz went into his woods, stopping every five feet to gasp for air.

He was greatly overweight as well as missing a hand. He hoped to reach his back fence an acre away and make his way to his store again before the heat of the afternoon sun burned him alive. He leaned against every tree in his path, and at every pause he fished for his breast-pocket handkerchief to wipe away his sweat. It was only when he was nearing the end of his property that he noticed a brown, sneakered leg poking out from among a set of tall ferns.

"Uh-oh," he said out loud. "That leg better be attached to someone."

Ruiz rushed to the girl's side. He crouched down beside her for a closer look. She was still breathing. She lay facedown in the dry bed of a rain creek, crusted blood matting her hair against her right temple, her right eye swollen shut. The skin of her face had turned from a light cinnamon to a dull purple, and it seemed distended, so that Ruiz thought for a moment that if he only dared to prick it with a needle her problems would be solved.

Other than a few leaves and seeds that stuck to them, her clothes were undisturbed. Lydia's left arm, tucked under her head as though she were reposing in sleep, had three long scratches on it.

Ruiz turned her over, using his stump as a lever.

"Come on girl. Get up," he whispered to her. He wanted to give her face light taps, but her skin color discouraged him.

"Come on, girl. I can't carry you. Get up." He prodded her hip.

Ruiz was right. He couldn't carry Lydia Fernandez back down the hill to his store. But after slapping her hands several times and waiting anxiously for half a minute, he tried to carry her anyway. He cradled her in his arms and sprang out of his crouch. The blood rushed to his head and, in his dizziness, he took a dozen steps downhill backwards before tripping over a fallen tree and sprawling onto the ground with the girl.

"¡Ay! ¡Ahora sí te maté!" he said. *Now I've killed you.*

Ruiz left Lydia where she lay and fell down once more while running back to his store. He called Jorge Nuñez from the phone kept under the store counter and gasped out his information, using his counter swipe to mop the sweat off his face and neck.

"I found her. Lydia. Behind my store. Get an ambulance. A doctor. She's hurt."

Nuñez made a hurried call to the clinic to have the sheriff meet him at Colmado Ruiz, then rushed to the town plaza.

After half an hour of looking, the ambulance driver finally found Angustias. Since there had no longer been a need for emergency medical services, he and his partner had parked near the town's plaza and were trying to finish the lunch they had started in Ponce.

"Come on," Nuñez said, banging on the hood of their vehicle. "We've got work for you. We found one of them."

"One of who?"

"One of the missing children."

"You have children missing?"

For Nuñez, there could be no news more important in the world than the fact that Samuel and Lydia were missing.

"Just follow my car."

Jorge led the ambulance to Colmado Ruiz. Gonzalo had met with his wife at the clinic, commandeered her car, and was already following the store owner uphill to where Lydia had been dropped. He helped the paramedics strap the girl onto a metal-framed canvas stretcher.

"Don't take her to Ponce," he said.

"We weren't going to. It's procedure. She goes to the nearest medical facility. There's a clinic around here, isn't there?"

"I'll take you," Nuñez said.

The paramedics and Nuñez made their way out of the relative cool of the forest. Gonzalo turned to Ruiz.

"Show me where she was."

Ruiz walked him over to the dry creek.

"She was lying there," he said, pointing to a large stone embedded at the edge of the creek.

"I think she was walking back here and fell on it," Ruiz added when Gonzalo remained silent. "Maybe she hit her head on the rock and was knocked out," he continued. "Maybe the dirt had dew on it, and she slipped when she—"

"Shut up, Ruiz. Just tell me exactly how you found her."

"Well, Nuñez called me at about—"

"No. Just tell me what position she was in when you first saw her."

Ruiz detailed Lydia's position when he had seen her. He even lay down on the rock in perfect mimicry.

"See, I'm telling you. She probably fell on the rock, hit her head, and got knocked out. She—"

"Then how come there's more bruising on the side that didn't hit the rock? The side that you say was faceup looks like it got smashed pretty hard. The skin is broken pretty good on that side. I'd say she was hit with a baseball bat. The other side, the facedown side, does look like she fell on this rock."

He crouched next to the rock.

"See? Here's a small bloodstain. She hit this rock with just enough force to get blood from her scalp. She fell here. This rock didn't give her the bruises on the right side."

From his crouch, he looked down along the creek bank. He imagined she had walked to this rock and collapsed on it after receiving a blow to the right side of her face.

"Get over here, Ruiz. Look for anything that might have caused the wound on the right side of her face—a bat, a rock . . ."

"A rock? There are a thousand rocks here."

"Yeah, but only one with blood on it."

"The big rock right next to you has blood on it."

"Don't be difficult. Another rock with blood on it."

It took only two minutes to find a second rock with blood on it a few steps farther down the creek. Ruiz brought it over to Gonzalo.

"This one has some blood on it."

Seeing the bloody rock with a single strand of hair the same length and shade as Lydia's in the store owner's hand, Gonzalo wanted to strangle the pudgy man. Instead, he rolled his eyes heavenward, looking at the patch of blue that broke through the dense foliage above, biting his tongue for all that he forgot to say when he involved Ruiz in the search for a weapon.

"What's the matter? Isn't this the rock you wanted? It was next to a coffee tree about twenty feet away. There's plenty of blood on the ground over there. . . ."

"No. You did fine. I'm mad at myself. I should have told you not to touch anything you find. This is a nice smooth stone. It's probably been in the creek for a thousand years. It has blood all over it. We can get a fingerprint off of it, but that print might be yours. See what I mean?"

"I didn't do anything to the girl."

"Relax. You're not a suspect. No one's accusing you of anything. But the evidence is a little tainted now. You understand me? Our case is a little weaker now."

Ruiz thought a moment.

"You want me to put it back?"

"No. Here. Just put it gently on this nice, flat rock here. Good. Now show me where you got the rock."

Ruiz walked the sheriff to a small clearing near the creek where, as he said, there was plenty of blood. There were also several candy wrappers and a soda can still half full and alive with ants. The attack on the girl was brutal but incomplete. She had been able to walk several yards to where she had fallen. Gonzalo stood silently for more than a minute.

"Who do you think did it?" Ruiz asked.

"I don't know. Could you let me think for a minute?"

Gonzalo didn't want to be short with Ruiz. It wasn't his usual manner, and he had never had any trouble with the store owner. They got along. In fact, Gonzalo felt a little guilty about the way Ruiz had lost his hand. If only he had responded to his frantic call for help a little sooner, driven a little faster, perhaps Ruiz would still have both hands. Gonzalo had acquitted himself well in the night-time gun battle outside the store as the criminals tried to leave. It was the most frightening experience he had endured in his years of police work—running around the store, through the store where the gunmen had killed one patron and maimed Ruiz, around the cars in the parking lot in front, into the woods behind. He had emptied his gun twice to stop three men. In the end, he had been grateful for the rain of that night. He was drenched, and no one could see he had wet his pants. Still, he had jumped out of his car just in time to hear the shotgun blast that had taken Ruiz's hand off. The man's business was nearly bankrupt, his common-law wife had left for San Juan; in every way, Raul Ruiz was close to ruin. No, Gonzalo didn't like being short with Ruiz, but then it had been a very long day.

"Go call my wife at the clinic. She's waiting for the Romans. Tell her I'm going to Comerio. I'll be sending Collazo over here. Don't touch anything or let anyone else up here, okay? When Collazo comes, show him where this is, okay? Go now. I'll be out of here in a minute."

Ruiz left, and Gonzalo looked up again at a patch of blue sky peeking at him through the leaves.

"What is it?" he asked the sky. "What is the answer? What is the reason for all this? I don't understand the message here. Is there a language of grief that I never learned? Is this the meaning of all mankind, of all creation? Is this the end? That we turn on the children and rape and kill and maim them? Explain this all to me," he prayed. "So I can go on and do my work and know where I'm going. Explain it to me."

Tears rolled down his face, off his chin, onto his shirt. The blue of the sky went uninterrupted, and after a moment of standing, waiting for a voice from above, he heard the birds again and the rustle of the leaves. This was no answer, but it reminded him that time was passing, and he had work to do. He glanced again at the sky, and he felt he had received a promise—no answers would be given, but he had the tools to find them himself. He trod out of the forest, back to his wife's car. Answers of another sort had to be sought in Comerio.

In the little clinic in Angustias, Mari Gonzalo was also searching for answers. When she got the news of Hector's chase and the Toyota's crash, she knew she would be the one to bring the information of Roberto Roman's death to his parents. As the sheriff's wife, she had learned to expect that some days would be truly endless for her; this was to be one of them.

Mari headed for the home of the Romans only to find Carmen Roman was not there. Agustin Martinez had already called her, and Carmen had headed for the school to pick up her daughter and get more information. After knocking several times, Mari got into her car and drove to the clinic. The Romans would end up there sooner or later; and she would be needed. Mari would show that the world cared for the loss suffered that day.

She sat down when she arrived. The mother of Roberto Roman was not in the lobby, not in sight.

"If you're looking for Carmen Roman, she's in with her boy already," the nurse told her a minute later.

Roberto Roman was laid out on a sofa in the doctor's office. His mother was kneeling beside him, holding his arm with one hand, brushing the hair from his face with the other. With each pass, Carmen outlined her son's misshapen forehead, caressed his discolored face. Her features alternated between anguish and calm, and her gaze was so intent that Mari was sure the grieving mother was trying to restore life with her look.

Mari stayed at the doorway for a full minute, but there was nothing for her to say or do. She returned to the hallway and sat waiting for Lydia and her mother. She did not leave her chair when she heard loud sobs come from the doctor's office a minute later. She had gone to the clinic to represent the world; but when she heard the crying, she was reminded that for that moment Carmen Roman's interest in the entire race of Man was negligible. What were all the species to her?

CHAPTER FOURTEEN

The first thing Collazo did when he arrived at Colmado Ruiz was make sure Ruiz knew there was to be no disturbing the site where Lydia had been found. Collazo went up the hill alone with his Polaroid and took pictures of the scene. He made note of the position of every candy wrapper and drop of blood. He took a brief statement from the store owner, and in twenty minutes he was back on the road. As long as the site wasn't disturbed, there would be time to return and more faithfully record the details of the area after the boy had been found.

He walked his way back down the hill and paused before entering the store to give Ruiz final instructions. He was almost dizzy from hunger. There was a slight burning sensation in the pit of his stomach that told him his body expected to be filled. He thought of asking Ruiz to fix him a sandwich, a little bread and butter with a cup of coffee maybe, just enough to hold him over, but the thought of Ruiz using his bandaged stump to help prepare the bread put him off. He gave Ruiz his instructions about guarding the scene while the man pushed a Snickers bar into his face. Collazo had never eaten a Snickers bar—he was an M&M man when he ate candy—but the chocolate made his mouth water.

"Remember. Make sure not a single soul goes up there without Gonzalo's permission. Only police, okay?"

"How am I supposed to keep people out if they want to go up there?"

"Tell them they can't. If they go up anyway, write their names down."

"What if they sneak on?"

"Well, maybe you should close up your store and take a chair up there. Read a magazine, take a radio. Just make sure no one touches anything up there, okay?"

"Close my store? I'll lose money. Is the city going to reimburse me for doing police work?"

While Ruiz had been holding the candy, Collazo spoke to him calmly. The last bit of Snickers disappeared before Ruiz spoke the last sentence, and Collazo became much less forgiving.

"Look. If that girl dies, there will be murder charges brought against the person who killed her. Believe me. You want the police on your side."

"Me? What about me? I didn't do anything to her!"

"I don't know. It's your land. You don't want to cooperate with the police. Gonzalo said your prints were on the weapon. You admitted to throwing her down the hill . . ."

"I fell! Look! I skinned my knees, my elbow, look!"

"Just guard the scene, Ruiz. It's better for everyone."

Collazo walked out to the sound of further nervous explanations. He felt a little guilty, but he saw Ruiz in his rearview mirror, closing the store and carrying a folding chair and a six-pack of beer toward the woods. In the rush of the next few hours, Raul Ruiz would be completely forgotten, and it was nearly midnight when he decided to walk off the hill and go to sleep, evidence be damned.

Meanwhile, Jorge Nuñez gave himself the task of bringing Lydia's mother to the clinic. There was no answer at the door. After a minute of knocking and calling, Nuñez tried the doorknob and found it ready to allow him entrance.

Inside, the house was dark. Most of the windows had been closed as though in preparation for nightfall, though it wasn't yet two in the afternoon. He left the door open behind him to admit the sunlight. The clutter in the living room amazed him. He had imagined that a mother and daughter living alone should have a house so neat it sparkled.

He called for Mrs. Fernandez, and she moaned in response. He looked around the room, certain the sound had come from somewhere near him. A pile of clothes and blankets on the sofa moved, and, realizing she was drunk, Jorge Nuñez yanked away all that covered Carmen Fernandez and tossed it on the floor. She lay naked on the sofa, shading her eyes but not bothering to cover any other part of herself. The deputy mayor jumped back about four feet in one step and gave the ceiling a firm, rebuking stare. He knew instantly that another man would have said something funny about the situation and left, but he couldn't think of anything humorous and couldn't get his feet to move any farther.

Carmen Fernandez jabbed him in the chest with her index finger.

"Who are you?" she asked. "Who gave you permission to come in here? Was it the girl? I'll kill that girl. Who are you?"

Nuñez looked down to respond to her, but instead of a face all he saw was a pair of breasts sagging to near flatness with nipples pointing to the floor as though they were the only parts of Carmen Fernandez to bow in shame. He looked up again.

"Doña Fernandez, I'm Jorge Nuñez. I'm the deputy mayor. I have information about—"

"She's dead!" Carmen screamed. "She's dead. I know it! I can feel it! In my heart!" she wailed.

She flung herself at Nuñez, throwing one arm around his neck. With her other hand she clutched Nuñez's right hand to her breast.

"I feel it in my heart!" she said.

Nuñez shoved her aside and ran for the door.

"She's not dead," he yelled from the safety of the doorway. "She's in the clinic. Put some clothes on; I'll drive you there. Just make sure you have something on before you come out to the car."

He wanted to yell something more about her drinking a cup of strong coffee, but Carmen Fernandez was in no condition to make her own coffee and he wasn't about to return to the house to make any for her. He decided to sit in his car however long it took her to dress. To his surprise, Carmen was out of the house in three minutes, wearing a sweatshirt and jeans, putting her hair into a ponytail with a comb and a rubber band. When she sat in the passenger seat next to him, he could see she had washed her face. Her breath smelled of coffee more than rum.

"What are you waiting for?" she said, and he drove to the clinic without further incident or mention of the incident that had passed.

At the clinic, Dr. Perez, Nurse Pagan, and Mari Gonzalo had found it impossible to keep Carmen Roman from confronting her son's abductor and killer. Carmen Roman was a small woman. She weighed a hundred pounds. A generous estimate would put her at five feet in height. When she announced, "I'm going to see this man," she could easily have been restrained. But then at that moment and ever since, her words and actions carried the force of an incalculable moral mass that none before her could resist. From the moment her son was murdered, her stature was increased to where she was unreachable by those around her. Tragedy does this to some. Great suffering inspires awe in onlookers so that they are afraid to touch the victim; sufferers gain veneration. As the saying goes, "The saints were none of them happy people."

Carmen Roman walked into Anthony Borden's room unopposed. The doctor, the nurse, and Mari watched her from the doorway. They instinctively felt that no one was a better judge of what Mrs. Roman should say or do than she was. She would not be hindered, no matter what course of action she decided on.

She stood at Anthony's bedside a full minute before he directed his gaze at her. The second he saw her, he began to cry; he understood who she was and what he had done to her; it was plain on her face. Her upper lip was streaked with mucus. Her eyes streamed tears; her breathing fluttered occasionally with a repressed sob. In her right hand there was a ball of tissue paper, soaked. This was the hand she raised, her index and middle fingers pointing at Anthony's face. It was a gesture that might have meant condemnation; the raised fingers seemed to accuse, but then she slowly lowered the fingers a half foot and half raised them again and finished the sign of a cross.

"Ego te absolvo," she said quietly.

She repeated the motion and the words twice more and looked at Anthony Borden a final time. She shook her head slowly and gave a short laugh as though he had done something disappointingly foolish, then left his room.

How she got out of the room was a mystery to the people who stood in the doorway. They swore they could not have moved out of her way from amazement over what she had done. But then, Carmen Roman is small and might have walked among them without their notice.

Carmen Fernandez's reaction to Anthony Borden was different. When Jorge Nuñez brought her into the clinic, Dr. Perez showed her into her child's room immediately. Carmen rushed toward the bed but stopped two feet short of it. She held her hands up before her in horror then balled them into fists. These fists she brought up to her mouth as though she were going to bite them. The doctor came near her and whispered into her ear.

"She's not as bad as she looks. She's breathing on her own. She's in a coma, but it is very light. We will snap her out of it in Ponce where they have better facilities. She's resting now, you see."

Carmen looked at the doctor slowly.

"Is she alright?"

"Well, she could be better of course. This is a very serious injury. . . ."

"Is she alright? Nuñez told me that the *americano* loves children. Is she alright?"

"He did nothing to her sexually. I'm not even sure he did this to her. I don't think so. He's a strong man. I mean, he was a strong man. I think if he wanted to kill her, he would have done it."

Carmen was not listening to any exculpations for Anthony Borden. In her mind, a man as sick as he was guilty of everything. She stooped over her child and caressed Lydia's face gently. She brushed hair away and whispered promises in the girl's ear.

"I will take care of you. I will protect you from now on. You will never need to worry about anything again. I will be there for all your needs," she whispered.

When she had passed a few minutes in this position, she got up and stormed out of the room and headed for the room where Anthony Borden lay. Her intent was clear. She wanted immediate retribution for what had happened to her daughter. Dr. Perez got in her way.

"Don't do this, Doña Carmen. Your daughter will be fine. Let the law handle this man—"

"This what?" she asked.

"This man—"

"You call that a man?" she said, her nostrils flaring, her brow knit in fury. "You call that a man? I don't call that a man. My husband was a man. You're a man. If I stepped on that thing in there, I wouldn't scrape my shoe on the wet grass, I would throw the shoe away. You understand me?"

"Yes, Doña Carmen. You're right. One hundred percent. I understand completely. But look. Your daughter needs you. If you do something to him, Gonzalo will have to arrest you—"

"What?"

"You know it is true. He might let you go the next day, but he will have to arrest you. Don't you want to be there when your daughter wakes up?"

Carmen Fernandez calmed a bit with that thought. Her tightly balled fists relaxed. Her breath began to come to her less convulsively.

"Let me see him," she said.

"What for?" Dr. Perez asked.

She glared at him.

"I didn't ask you to interrogate me. I'm not going to kill him, okay? I won't even touch him. I just want that thing to look at me."

The doctor relented. He guided her to the doorway.

"Hey," she yelled at Borden.

He turned his eyes toward her slightly.

"You are nothing," she said in Spanish. Then she spat at him, the saliva landing on his forehead and running down to his pillow. As Gonzalo had predicted, no one bothered to clean him.

Carmen Fernandez returned to her daughter's room and took a seat against a wall. She was determined to be the first vision her daughter saw upon awaking. After a few minutes, Carmen Fernandez fell asleep in her vigil, and Mari thought it best to return to Isabel Villareal. Having given Gonzalo her car, she borrowed Irma Pagan's yellow hatchback to drive to the Villareal home.

Miguel Roman came in a little later. Roberto's father was brought by Agustin Martinez, who had sought him out and taken him early from work. Miguelina Roman rode silent in the backseat. When the two men left the car and entered the clinic, she stayed behind. No one had thought to blame her for the events of the day. She didn't need anyone's blame to feel that her brother's death was her fault.

Miguel Roman searched for his wife, and they spent some minutes crying in each other's arms in the hallway. The doctor and nurse had no idea what to do with themselves. There was no place for them to excuse themselves to without edging past the grieving couple.

When, after viewing the lifeless body of his son with its misshapen head, distended belly, and olive complexion, Miguel Roman decided to pay Anthony Borden a visit, no one even moved to stop him. Like his wife, he was thought to have a right to exact justice on the man who had so clearly wronged him.

Anthony Borden was already crying when Miguel entered his

room. Miguel stood at his bedside, thinking of what to do. Coming face to face with his son's killer was different in feeling than anything he had imagined. Had he been asked a day or year earlier what he would have wanted at that precise moment, he would have responded without hesitation.

"I would kill the man who laid a hand on Robertito."

His path was so clear while it remained mere speculation, that the reality of his current situation seemed a chimera. Miguel laughed at himself. He pointed at Borden and continued laughing. Though he was crying for his son at the same time, he could not stop his laughter, and the laughter seized him so that he doubled over with pain in his side.

He left the room when his laughing had subsided enough to allow him to straighten up.

"If I am confused," he told Borden as he left. "If I am confused, imagine what is going on in your head," he said, and he laughed himself out of the room.

CHAPTER FIFTEEN

Driving to Comerio, Gonzalo wondered if he should stop to find a lawyer to take with him; the accused might demand a counselor, and it would interrupt the flow of questioning to seek one once the interview had begun. He decided against taking one with him. It was worth trying to get Poole to talk before a lawyer got involved. Criminals often thought they could outsmart the police and revealed valuable information as they tried to clear themselves. Also, he didn't want to have to explain Poole's crimes to a third party unless it was unavoidable.

In the few minutes it took to get to Comerio, he tried to work out a tack for questioning Poole. It seemed clear that he had had nothing to do with Lydia's beating, but nothing so far cleared him in the disappearance of Samuel Villareal. The picture Gonzalo carried in his breast pocket seemed to make it more likely that Poole would fancy a boy Samuel's age. The picture was evidence enough to get Poole convicted of just about anything, but that wouldn't help get Samuel back. Gonzalo wondered which persona he could develop, what line of questions he could take that would be most effective in getting the suspect to share what useful information he had.

Because this was Comerio, because of Sheriff Molina's naturally violent disposition, Gonzalo decided he would act the part of good cop. He would explain to Poole all the benefits of cooperating. He would highlight the harsh treatment he could expect if he remained Molina's prisoner. He didn't doubt Molina had already made himself unpleasant to Poole—it never took Molina more than a few seconds to annoy Gonzalo. The suspect might already be willing to say anything to get away from the sheriff of Comerio.

Two officers in bulletproof vests and helmets stood guard outside the precinct. One of them trained his shotgun on Gonzalo as he came up the stairs. Gonzalo smacked the barrel away.

"Aim that thing at me again, and I'll make you sorry. Where's Molina? Inside?"

Molina was at his desk.

"I'm pretty upset with you." He jabbed his finger at Gonzalo. "I just spent the last hour on the phone with the FBI in Washington, D.C. You know how much that bill's going to come out to? Then it turns out this guy isn't even a *Machetero*. He's a nobody. Spent eight years in jail for something forty years ago—"

"Eight years for what?"

"Huh? I don't know. Something. Anyway, he's not a *Machetero*—"

"I know. He's a pedophile."

"Yeah. Something like that is what the FBI guy said. What is it?"

"Believe me. You don't want to know."

"Sure I do. That's why I asked."

Gonzalo took the picture from his shirt pocket and tossed it onto Molina's desk. Molina pulled open his lap drawer and retrieved a pair of glasses. With these on, he picked up the picture carefully and stared at it. It was a full minute before he could speak.

"That kid's my grandson's age," he said.

"I know. There are a lot of people who can say that. But right now, I have to worry about another little boy. I have to worry about Samuel Villareal. Are you with me on this? You understand I need information more than anything else. If this guy knows where that boy is, I need to know it. Are you listening to me?"

Sheriff Molina was staring at a non-existent point somewhere beyond Gonzalo.

"Molina. You with me on this? I need this guy to cooperate. I need him to talk to me."

"I'll get him to talk," Molina said.

"No. We can't afford to alienate him."

"Alienate? What's that? I don't plan to do anything fancy. That boy could be my grandson. I'm gonna take that old bastard and make him beg for a bullet in the brain—"

"No. I need him talking, not dead."

"He'll talk. He'll tell me anything you need. Alienate. Huh. You college guys come up with words from nowhere. I'll alienate the shit out of this guy."

Gonzalo put a hand to his forehead. He had been speaking with Molina for two minutes, and he could sense a headache coming on. Molina made a move to come out from behind his desk, and Gonzalo put his hand to the gun in its holster. Molina froze and smiled.

"What? Now you're going to shoot a cop over this guy? Believe me. It ain't worth it, Gonzalo."

"I don't plan to shoot a cop at all. Whatever I do, it isn't for the guy you have back there. If I do anything, it's because I need to find Samuel. You understand me?"

Molina put his hands up in a conciliatory gesture.

"I got you."

"You with me on this?"

"I'm with you. You want to try some psychology on this guy? Fine. I'll tell you one thing I can see from him. This guy's a wise guy. He thinks he's smarter than everyone. If you don't put the fear of God in him, he ain't gonna give you nothing. Anyway. You want to dance around with him, go ahead. Let me know when you're done. Then he's mine, okay?"

"Fine. Whatever. I just need to get some information."

Molina walked Gonzalo to the cells in the back and brought the prisoner to an interrogation room. When Poole had taken his seat, hands still cuffed behind him, Gonzalo walked into the room. "What is all this?" Poole asked. Molina laughed as he opened the door to leave. "Hee gana 'alien' yu," he laughed out in his best English. With the door closed, the interrogation room was dark and smelled of sweat and urine. Besides the table and four heavy, wooden chairs, there was no furniture. A single light fixture hung from the ceiling, of the kind usually only seen in the type of old private-eye movie where a cigarette hangs from the corner of every mouth and the police are called "coppers." Gonzalo took a quick glance around the room before taking a seat across from Poole. There were no windows, and the walls looked quite solid. There was no recording equipment, and Gonzalo wondered if the room was soundproof. "Silly question," he said out loud.

"What?" Poole responded.

"Nothing, nothing. I need to ask you a few simple questions—"

"I want a lawyer. I'll tell you right now, I am fully aware of my rights. I won't say anything without a lawyer."

David Poole turned his face away from Gonzalo.

"Look, Mr. Poole, we need a certain piece of information from you . . ."

"Look, sheriff, you can ask anything you want. I won't answer a thing without a lawyer. I know my rights. You're not dealing with some punk teenager off the street. Now, go get me a phone and a phone book."

Poole turned his head again.

Gonzalo took a seat opposite the suspect.

"Okay, Mr. Poole. You don't want to talk without a lawyer? That's fine. You do have that right. But if you don't want to talk, I think you should at least listen. Okay?"

Poole turned his face back to Gonzalo.

"Good. Now here are the facts pertaining to your incarceration. Today is Friday. You will be kept here until you can be brought before a judge in San Juan for arraignment. There are weekend courts, but it is at the discretion of Sheriff Molina whether to go tomorrow or Monday. Frankly, there's a better selection of judges on Monday. You understand?"

"Yes."

"Good. Now you will be fed three meals a day—essentially sandwich, coffee, sandwich, coffee, sandwich, coffee. You understand?"

"Yes."

"Good. My English is not too great."

"Your English is fine."

"Thank you. Now. When you are brought before the judge, you

will be charged with, among other things, conspiracy to kidnap with the intention of doing harm, assault on an officer with a deadly weapon (that might turn into attempted murder, I'm not quite sure yet), and the murder of the kidnap victim—"

"Murder?"

"Oh, certainly. Roberto Roman's head was crushed. His neck was snapped. His internal organs were jarred loose. His blood pooled in his belly, which swelled as though he had swallowed a basketball. You were part of a conspiracy, part of the actions that brought all this about. We call that murder. You understand?"

"Yes."

"In any event, Anthony Borden will testify to all of this. I'm sure he can explain it in such a way that your exact role will be clear to all."

"Anthony Borden?"

"Certainly. He told us all about you. He survived the crash, but just barely. Broken neck. He'll never walk again. Anyway, with all these charges, not to mention your attempted escape from here . . ."

"Attempted escape? What do you mean, attempted escape? I haven't tried anything."

"Not yet. Everyone tries to escape from here if Molina dislikes them. He makes sure of it. Molina hates you more than any other criminal he's ever dealt with, I can promise you that. Believe me; attempted escape will be one of the charges, but don't worry. That's a charge Molina might drop. No matter. I guarantee you no bail, a speedy trial, and a jail cell from now until the end of your days. Not to say that you will never see sunshine again, Mr. Poole, but once you're put in solitary confinement, you won't see the sun again until they wheel you out on a gurney to go to the hospital. You understand me?"

"Yes."

"Good. Now I can help you . . ."

"How did I know you were going to say that?"

"I don't know. Maybe you're psychic. Anyway, I can help you, but I need the location of a little boy, Samuel Villareal. He was taken last night sometime after nine. If you cooperate, if we get the boy back unharmed, we might be able to downplay your role in the death of Roberto Roman this afternoon. You understand?"

"Sure. Now you listen to me. I'm not just some little punk you picked up off the street. I know my rights. I don't know any Samuel Villawhatever, and I have nothing to say to you without a lawyer. I'm not afraid of you. Now, do you understand me?"

Poole puffed out his chest and straightened himself in his chair. Gonzalo leaned back and let out a deep breath.

"Mr. Poole, I don't think you understand that you will be going to jail for the rest of your life, guaranteed, no mistake about it, whether or not you have a lawyer. That's if you don't cooperate. If you help me find Samuel, you have a chance of going to a prison in America. You have a chance of getting out in ten years. If you don't cooperate, I can't do anything for you."

"Tell it to my lawyer. I'm not listening, Mr. Gonzalo."

Poole turned in his chair.

"Okay. So you don't want to talk and now you don't want to listen. Fine. Then just look."

Gonzalo took the picture from his shirt pocket and tossed it onto the table in front of Poole. He expected to see the man's face turn pale or perhaps an even brighter shade of red. Instead, nothing happened. Poole leaned forward to take a closer look at the photo.

"I want my lawyer," he said and turned away again.

Gonzalo thought a minute. He couldn't see how Poole was able to remain calm when the clearest evidence of unforgivable sin had just been presented to him. "For goodness sakes," Gonzalo thought. "Even I'm blushing at that picture."

He folded the photo back into his breast pocket, then left the room. In another minute, he was back with Molina.

"Sheriff Molina. I've been trying to explain to Mr. Poole that he should help me. I'm offering him a chance to have his sentence reduced, to face lesser charges. Can you add anything to persuade him to help?"

Molina put his fists on the table and leaned toward the suspect.

"I keel yu," he hissed out between his teeth.

Poole laughed in the sheriff's face.

"Go away. I've seen better 'good cop/bad cop' routines on *Starsky and Hutch*. You think you scare me? Please. Get me a lawyer. I know my rights better than you guys do."

Poole continued laughing, and Gonzalo took hold of one of Molina's arms, pulling him gently out of the room.

"What do you think?" Gonzalo asked outside.

"Same as before. You're not gonna get anything from him that way. You go continue looking for that boy. One of my deputies said he found out the guy had a hideout on one of the hills here in Comerio. I sent two guys to collect evidence. I'm headed there now; wanna come along?"

"No. You guys can handle this. You know what to do if you find the boy or some hint about where he is?"

"Let me guess. You want to know, right?"

"Yep. You know how to find me. I'll be in Angustias continuing the search. Collazo will be in the fields."

"How is the old guy? Haven't seen him in weeks."

"Collazo? Looks the same."

"Hey. One last thing. Anything special about *el gringo*? You want him?"

"Nope. He's yours. If he gives you anything about the boy, let me know. That's all I care about."

Gonzalo left the station house and got back into his car. He felt that Poole had nothing to do with the disappearance of Samuel Villareal. This should have been a good thing, but for some reason the feeling weighed upon his mind heavily. He drove away wondering if he would ever see the little boy again.

Molina went out into the fields of Comerio with his men. Once the news of the crash in Angustias and the arrest in the gas station began to spread, everyone remembered seeing the two Toyotas and their drivers. Everyone would have said something sooner had they known it was important. To everyone, Poole and Borden had been no more than two tourists passing through, possibly lost. Poole had stopped at a grocery store for Twinkies. Borden had explained to one child that he was a land developer; the hill with the shacks was finally going to be a radio tower, people thought. A man traveling with them, a Puerto Rican, had bought a puppy for five dollars. Once it was newsworthy, everyone in town could discuss the two drivers at length and in detail.

The hilltop yielded nothing of consequence to the search for Samuel Villareal. Molina got Gonzalo on his CB only fifteen minutes into the search to report this. There was little that was of any immediate use among the shacks. There was a small satchel with more pictures—Poole with other boys, Anthony Borden with a boy, boys with each other. There was also extra clothing for Poole in the satchel and a passport and nameless vouchers for tickets from San Juan to London and about six thousand dollars. Molina dumped everything into his car trunk.

A closer inspection of the site revealed that one shack had been used extensively, perhaps as a command center of some sort. There were sets of footprints belonging to three men. One of the shacks had a padlock. Molina had it clipped off to find nothing but a pile of thick blankets. His deputies were disappointed, but Molina imagined this was where Roberto Roman would have been kept until he could be taken off the island. A wave of outrage welled within him, blinding him. He grabbed the broken lock still dangling off the doorjamb. He gave it a twist and a pull and tore it off the post. He squeezed the metal in his fist, squeezing harder when a torn edge of the lock bit into his palm and three or four drops of blood in quick succession came out between his tight-wound fingers and fell to the dirt below. He stormed off toward his car.

"There are three car tracks here, boss," one deputy said, approaching him.

"Tell Gonzalo." He walked on.

"You going in, boss?"

Molina stopped and the deputy who had gotten to within a yard of him instinctively jumped back. Molina jabbed the index finger of his right hand, the hand with the lock and the blood, into the deputy's face.

"I'm gonna talk to *el gringo ese*. Okay? You're gonna stay here. You're gonna investigate every inch of this place. You're gonna get Gonzalo on the CB and tell him everything you found. You're gonna stay up here until I tell you to come down or you'll be sorry. You got all that? Was it too much for you? No? Good. Now don't say another word."

It was uncommon for Molina to talk roughly to his deputies. He had been an enlisted man in the army and would have no distance between him and his men if possible. Still, though he usually saved his threats for criminals, only a fool would have tested his patience just then.

Molina drove with fury off the hill. He didn't even know how to ask forgiveness for the visions that clouded and corrupted his mind's eye. Every time he blinked, he saw Poole naked on the thick blankets with a child doing things, forcing things that would shame even an animal.

He called in ahead to the station house.

"Where's the prisoner?"

"In his cell."

"I want him in the conference room. I want everyone out when I get there. I want six guys in Angustias; find Collazo. He's probably in the Valley; help in the house-to-house. The rest I want on Sierra Las Batatas. Calderon and Rivera are there now. There are tire tracks. I want to know where they go. You got me? I want the station empty when I get there."

"But we arrested José Maldonado for drunkenness. . . ."

"Did you not hear me? I want the place empty. Empty. Me and Poole. That's it. Release Maldonado. Take him home."

"Okay, boss."

A minute or two later, when Molina entered the station house, the front room was silent. The cells in the back had been vacated, and one conference-room door was open, the other closed. Molina moved to his desk and rifled through the lap drawer. He selected several items, then stopped to look slowly around the room. The moment was an epiphany; at the age of fifty-five, Molina came to understand his life. Everything from his playground fights to the 29 tattooed onto his forearm to mark his confirmed kills in Korea, everything began to make some sense. Not perfect sense—life is too short for that, perhaps—but some sense. He had begun his survey of the room thinking that the universe, represented by every phone and desk and chair, had betrayed him. Poole was such an aberration that the world itself seemed corrupt and foul because he was in it. But by the time Molina looked back down at the items on his desk, he understood. Every fight, every scar, every bone broken by him and in him had helped to harden him for this day. If Poole was an aberration, Molina saw himself as all that was needed to make things right.

He gathered his items into a crumpled paper bag and went in to meet Mr. Poole.

"It's about time." Poole said as Molina closed the door behind himself. "I've had these cuffs on since twelve-thirty." Molina ignored his prisoner and made sure the door was locked. *"¡Quítanme las esposas!"* Poole shouted in frustration. *Take off the handcuffs.*

Molina looked at him in dull surprise.

"So you speak Spanish?" he said.

"Yes. Now take these cuffs off, my arms are killing me."

"Okay," Molina said, and he moved behind Poole and undid the handcuffs. Poole stretched and rubbed his shoulders. He spoke to Molina in Spanish with a thick but understandable accent.

"Good," he said. "Now this is a little progress. I want to speak to a lawyer. I know my rights."

The sheriff moved to his paper bag on the other side of the table, ignoring Poole again.

"You can't just ignore me. I know you understand me. My Spanish isn't that bad."

"Sit down, Mr. Poole. You don't have the right to a lawyer here."

"What?"

"You have the right to have your hands free. You have the right to a seat, unless you really prefer to stand for this; I grant you that. But you don't have the right to a lawyer, not here."

"What do you mean, 'not here'? I'm an American citizen—"

"This is not America."

"Puerto Rico is a part of the U.S. What do you think I am? Stupid?"

"This is not Puerto Rico," Molina said calmly.

"What are you talking about? Are you drunk?"

"It's simple, Mr. Poole. We're not in America. We're not in Puerto Rico. We're in Comerio. We're in my town, in my house. So defend yourself. You'll only get one chance."

"What? You planning to beat me up? I can take you." Poole laughed at what he meant to be a joke, but it was a nervous laugh.

Molina took a seat across the table from the prisoner.

"You are a predator—you hunt children, you follow them, you capture them, you abuse them and sell them. All I want to know is why you do this."

Poole sat back in his chair and smiled. The smile turned into a soft chuckle, and he was about to chide Molina about this horrible attempt at getting a confession, but the sheriff lunged across the table, grabbed Poole's throat, knocking him over in his chair, and landing on his chest. Before the first words of his response had formed in Poole's head, Molina had broken his nose. He was about to scream, "You broke my nose," but Molina was busy administering a dozen more punches and would not have heard him anyway.

The sheriff of Comerio got off the suspect's chest and got a length of duct tape and a black, foot-long electric stun gun from his paper bag, and Poole could think of nothing else to say.

CHAPTER SIXTEEN

At two o'clock, Gonzalo and Collazo met in the shade of a bread-fruit tree along the side of the main highway in the Valley. They would have passed each other going in opposite directions, but Gonzalo flagged his deputy down. Except for calls on the CB and a message or two relayed by third parties, he hadn't really touched base with this deputy since meeting him at the crash site of the red Toyota.

The early forecast of ninety-two degrees seemed ridiculous to both men. It was at least that hot in the shade.

"Anything?" Gonzalo asked.

"About the boy? No. I would have gotten you on the CB if there was a good lead."

"What about a bad lead?"

"I don't bother you with garbage."

"Do you check them out?"

"I've checked out a couple. Doña Carmela said she heard noises on her property every night for the last few days. I took a machete and cut my way around her property; no one's cut a weed on her land since her husband died. That's a pity. It's very nice land. . . ."

"Find anything?"

"Sure. Three dogs: a bitch in heat and two *machos*. The male that was waiting his turn actually tried to scare me off. I guess he thought I was going to try to cut in line."

"What'd you do?"

"Gave him a good whack in the teeth with the nightstick."

"You said there was another lead?"

"Yup. Don Santiago said he saw the boy. I talked to him fifteen minutes before I was sure he only wanted some attention. Didn't even know what the child looked like."

"How old is Don Santiago?"

"Santiago's younger than I am; seventy at most. He just spent his life cheating people and doesn't have a soul who'll spend an hour with him."

"That's what you get when you think about money before people."

"Yup."

"Now. You said you checked out two of the bad leads. Were there any other bad leads?"

"Well, there was something the boy said that stuck in my mind, but I was planning to check it out when we got really desperate."

"I'm desperate now, Collazo. Give me what you have, and I'll check it out."

"You sure?"

"Right now, I don't have anything even remotely promising."

"Okay then. Hector said something about talking to one person in the time before he got shot at. Julio Chagara came up behind him when he was yelling out the child's name and said, '*Samuel no está.*' Julio lives pretty high up in the hills, so I doubt the boy could have passed anywhere near his house. Still, Julio does go to the Protestant church sometimes, so he should know who Samuel is."

"Julio goes to the Protestant church?"

"Yup. They give him things to do. He told me they let him play the *güiro,* and he's allowed to stay in the children's class. He helps them put away chairs, things like that. You sure you want to talk to Julio? I can do it, if you want. I just wasn't going to make it a priority."

Gonzalo thought for a while. Interviewing Julio Chagara on this matter would be like discussing politics with a four-year-old. He was inclined to let Collazo conduct this interview.

"Well," he said. "What were you planning to do right now?"

"I was heading into town," Collazo answered.

"What for?"

"Well, I haven't eaten breakfast or lunch, and I was hoping to—"

"Oh my God. I'm sorry, *viejo.* I just ate a sandwich myself. I would have gotten you one. I wasn't thinking. Go. Go into town. Get some food. This might be a long day for us. I'll talk to Chagara."

"You sure?"

"Yes. Go, go."

The two men went their separate ways.

Collazo had no intention of getting a sandwich for himself. That could not be considered a proper lunch. Instead he was going to a tiny diner only a hundred yards from the center of town. Cafetín Lolita was an establishment so immune to busyness and hurry, so un-

mindful of provoking interest or attention, that it was clearly await-
ing the death of the proprietress so it could be gutted and renovated
and given new life as something, anything, useful to the young. This
is where Collazo headed for his lunch. And why not? Lolita Gomez
was a woman of his generation and the food was good.

The only thing that told a visitor that they were approaching
Cafetín Lolita was the fact that there were remnants of the painted
name on the large plate-glass window in front. Unlike other eatery
owners, Lolita didn't bother to post any menus in the window (her
customers knew what was available), nor did she list any specials of
the day (there were none). When asked about prices, she usually assured people her prices were *regular,* that is, average. This vagueness
veiled the fact that prices had never been set—Lolita reserved the
right to charge as much as she felt a meal was worth on that particular day. Clearly, making soup on a hot and humid day was more
difficult than on a cool day; the price reflected this. Lolita also
needed the flexibility to charge more when she needed money.

Inside, the diner was spare. There was a Formica-topped counter
with four stools. Behind that, there was a partition that set the
kitchen apart from the rest of the restaurant. Most customers sat at
the counter, ignoring the four tables and eight chairs that comprised
the rest of the diner.

Collazo took the last available seat at the counter when he entered. The other three patrons were men he had known all his life,
but he did not feel comfortable with the company. Conversation had
halted as he walked in through the door. Samuel Villareal was no
doubt the subject at hand, and the only reference to Collazo would
have been on his failure to find the boy. He wanted to defend himself, to explain exactly how much acreage there was to cover, how
many houses and sheds, to explain that the boy might not even be in

Angustias or on the island anymore. He wanted to show the hornet stings on his arm; he wanted to roll down his socks to show where a dozen *hormigas bravas,* wild ants, had attached themselves to his leg. He wanted to explain that he hadn't eaten since the night before, that he hadn't really slept in more than twenty-four hours. Most of all, he wanted to tell his fellow diners that the disappearance of Samuel Villareal wasn't his fault; he had done nothing *to* the boy; he was trying to do something *for* the boy. But he couldn't see the relevance to any of these arguments. No one had attacked him yet, but even if they did, the essential fact remained—the boy had not yet been found.

It was only after he had ordered his plate of rice, beans, fried chicken drumsticks, and *tostones* with a tall glass of ice water—a traditional Puerto Rican lunch—that the questions began.

"Anything on that boy yet?" one of the patrons asked.

"Nope," Collazo said.

He folded and refolded the napkin in front of him, anticipating the arrival of his food.

"Any clues?"

"Nope."

"Any connection to the boy that got stolen from the school?"

"Don't know."

"Was it the *Macheteros*?"

"Don't know."

"What do you know?"

Collazo thought for a minute. It wasn't his custom to divulge the facts of a case to those not directly involved in it. But then, that's what he had been doing for hours, knocking on the doors of people who had no connection to the case, explaining the situation, getting permission to search their properties.

"I know the boy's name is Samuel Villareal. He's six years old.

179

He was last seen at nine last night wearing slippers and shorts that reach his knees."

"I know the kid you're talking about," said the man at the far end of the counter. Collazo was somewhat surprised at this since the man lived in town, far from the Valley.

"Yeah. The father's as skinny as a stick, right?"

"Yeah."

"And the mother doesn't go to any of the church parties—no *fiestas patronales,* no Three Kings' Day, no nothing. . . ."

"She doesn't go to Catholic church at all," Collazo said.

"What do you mean?" the man asked. "Even I go, though it's only on the days when there's a party. Everyone goes to church."

"The family is Protestant," Collazo explained.

"Protestant? What's that? Like Jehovah's Witness?" the man asked.

Collazo was about to answer "No," but now that it had been mentioned, he wondered what the correct answer was.

Lolita came from the kitchen with Collazo's food.

"Protestants are like Jews and Muslims," she said. "They don't believe in anything. They believe in Martín Calvino."

"Who?" the first man asked.

"Martín Calvino. He was a priest in America about a thousand years ago. I think he preached to the Indians."

Collazo was sure this information was false, but he was too hungry to argue.

"What does all this have to do with the boy?" he asked between mouthfuls. "If you have anything to say about him, say it."

"Oh, well, we were all saying that you should talk to his sister's boyfriend. That *señorito* thinks he owns the world. If anyone did anything to the little kid, it was probably that girl's boyfriend."

"What's the boy's name?"

"Who?"

"The boyfriend."

"Oh, I don't know. That's what we were all trying to figure out when you came in. He's a bad one. He may not have done anything bad yet, but you can tell he will someday."

"But you can't tell me anything specific about him? Is he tall or short, fat or skinny? Anything?"

"That's just the thing," one of the patrons said. "He's not anything special. We just know him by the way he struts around. He walks like he owns Angustias."

This, of course, wasn't much of a description.

"Well, which of Samuel's sisters is dating this kid?"

"How many sisters does he have?" Lolita asked.

"Two."

"Oh. Well, this sister has long, dark hair."

"They both do."

"Oh. Well, why don't you ask the mother? She should know which has a boyfriend."

Collazo finished his lunch. He agreed that a mother should know when her daughter has a boyfriend, but he realized this was only rarely the case. Still, this was something to report to Gonzalo. Another less than fulfilling lead.

Meanwhile, Gonzalo was trying to find Julio Chagara. Normally, Julio was quite easy to find. He lived in a one-room shack, and Gonzalo checked on him once a week. Most times, there was nothing more to finding Julio than to park on the side of the road and climb along a well-worn footpath, uphill to the shack. The home wasn't visible from the road, but the path didn't allow for deviation; on either side there was grass that surpassed Gonzalo's height. At the end of the path there was a tiny wooden home, sitting on stilts, embedded in a grove of fruit trees. Julio was usually in a hammock strung up inside the house. He spent hours rocking himself with one foot on the floor, and he listened to a portable radio. The news station was his favorite, though he sometimes lost his place on the dial. On this occasion, the hammock was empty.

Gonzalo did a quick turn around the house, checked the latrine, then started calling out. There was no response. On a second turn around the shack, Gonzalo spotted a second footpath leading downhill away from the house. It led Gonzalo to the road again a few dozen feet from where he had parked his car. Across the road, the path continued farther downhill, and Gonzalo followed it.

Julio was at the end of the trail, sitting on a boulder that jutted out of the side of the hill. The rock was smooth, as though it had been washed in a river for a few centuries. This struck Gonzalo as curious since there wasn't a flowing source of water anywhere nearby, but that wasn't his concern at the moment.

Gonzalo stood behind Julio and looked off in the direction of Julio's gaze. He saw nothing of note. As far as the eye could see, the view was of heavily forested hills sparsely dotted with homes. Apparently, Julio had chosen the spot for the beauty of the landscape it presented and its quietness.

Gonzalo cleared his throat and gently called Julio by his full name, but he got no response. Julio continued staring at the mountains of Puerto Rico's Cordillera Central.

"Julio, I need to talk to you," Gonzalo said, touching Julio on the shoulder. Julio turned to face him, startled. He whipped a black headset off his ears.

"I'm sorry, Julio. I didn't mean to scare you. What's that you had on your head?" Gonzalo asked.

"It's called Sony. Father Perea gave it to me on my birthday."

"Oh. I've seen those advertised. They play tapes and radio, right?"

Julio answered nothing.

"How do they sound? I've been thinking of getting one."

Julio offered him the headset and the Walkman. Gonzalo put the headset on and fidgeted with the Walkman.

"Julio, this isn't on. This doesn't even have batteries in it. What were you listening to?"

Julio shrugged. "When you put it on, it makes everything sound different," he said.

Gonzalo handed back the set and made a mental note to himself to return with batteries and a tape or two.

"I need to ask you a few questions about Samuel Villareal. Is that okay, Julio?"

"*Samuel no está,*" Julio said.

"Exactly. Who told you Samuel is lost?"

"He's not lost."

"Where is he?"

Julio pointed to the hill across from his position.

"He's in Doña Perfecta's house?" Gonzalo asked.

"Not there. There," Julio said, shifting his arm a bit.

"In her *casita de café*?" Gonzalo said.

Julio's index finger seemed aimed at a small wooden shack with a new zinc roof less than a hundred yards away from Doña Perfecta's home.

Julio nodded.

"How do you know?"

"I saw him. A girl put him in there."

"What girl?"

"I don't know. Long hair."

"You saw that from here?"

"Not from here. From there." Julio pointed again.

"You were in Doña Perfecta's house?"

Julio shook his head no.

"Where were you?" It was a bit difficult for Gonzalo to remember not to ask "yes or no" questions.

"Near the car, but not too near. Nobody saw me, but I saw them."

This response was less than helpful. In Gonzalo's mind, chances were slight that Samuel Villareal had been put in the shack Doña Perfecta used for storing her picked coffee beans. It was nearly five miles by road from Samuel's home; two miles through the woods, but they would have been difficult to cross in the dark. There was also the fact that Doña Perfecta didn't have a car. She had never learned to drive in her eighty years. Still, he had come to check on a lead, and he decided to follow it to its end.

"Come on, Julio. Let's get in my car."

"Where are we going?" Julio asked. He got up and started following Gonzalo up the footpath.

"We're going to Doña Perfecta's house."

Julio stopped in midstep.

"Is he still there?" he asked.

Gonzalo sighed and ignored him. As he helped Julio buckle his seat belt, he estimated that the entire trip to Doña Perfecta's house and back, including a search of the little shack, would take fifteen minutes. Then he could get back to police work.

CHAPTER SEVENTEEN

The first sign of trouble at Doña Perfecta's house was that the gate in the fence around her property, three rusted strands of barbwire stretched across a frame of rough-hewn saplings, had been broken loose off one of its hinges. By itself, this was not significant; the gate had been in place for as long as Gonzalo could remember. It was about time it fell off. It did not take long, however, for him to notice other signs of trouble.

The two men got out of the car and crossed onto Doña Perfecta's land.

"He broke the fence," Julio said.

"Samuel?"

"No. The other one."

"The girl?"

"No. He, he. I said 'he.' The man with the car."

Julio pointed down to the short grass, which was matted in such a way as to make it clear a car had passed recently.

"Stay where you are," Gonzalo said, and Julio froze near the gate.

Gonzalo moved toward the house, watching his step, making sure not to disturb any other tracks.

The white, metal slat windows were rolled shut at the front of the house. This was another irregularity. Many closed their windows at night but opened the ones in the shade when the sun came out. Gonzalo knew this was part of Doña Perfecta's morning ritual just as it was for all her neighbors.

Three cinder blocks cemented together formed two steps up to the front entrance of the house.

"Doña Perfecta," Gonzalo called at the door.

No one answered, and, after a minute's wait, Gonzalo gently pushed the unlocked door open.

Inside, as expected, there was almost nothing. In the living room, there was a lone chair facing a small television that sat on a little TV cart. In the bedroom, there was a twin-size bed and opposite the foot of the bed, a few feet away, there was a four-drawer bureau.

After quick looks through these rooms, Gonzalo headed for the back door in the kitchen. The clearest sign of trouble was on the kitchen floor. The very tip of Gonzalo's shoe touched the dry remains of a small pool of blood. Seeing the spot with his peripheral vision, he pulled up short. There was a trail of smeared blood heading out the door. Gonzalo was about to follow the trail out when his peripheral vision revealed another interesting image. His took his ballpoint pen out of his breast pocket and stooped to examine the thin lock of long black-and-gray hair resting near the stove.

The strands were attached to a half-dollar-size piece of flesh; part of Doña Perfecta's scalp had been cut away. Gonzalo reached for the gun in his holster. He felt unsafe suddenly, though the killing had happened many hours before, and the killer was most likely long gone. A thought for Julio standing alone and unprotected outside flashed through the sheriff's mind. He put the image out of his head and took his hand off his gun. There was a killer loose, but Julio was safe in the open.

Gonzalo followed the trail of blood out the back door onto the grass at the side of the house. The trail ended at just that point where the car tracks came to a stop. There were signs that the car had backed up after having parked for a long enough time to make substantially deeper impressions than all the rest of the tracks. A few feet farther down, there were signs of a three-point turn. Presumably, the body had been dumped into the trunk of a car and driven off.

Gonzalo looked to Julio, still at the gate.

"Stay there," he yelled.

Julio nodded vigorously, and Gonzalo started to make his way toward the coffee shack. He looked toward the sun and wanted nothing more than for the day to be done. It had been filled with shocks, and he told himself as he approached the little wooden structure that he would no longer be surprised to find Samuel Villareal in the shack as Julio had said. At this point, he would not be surprised to find Santa Claus sitting on a sack of coffee beans in there.

"Samuel!" he called out while still a few yards away. There was no answer.

The door to the shack was bolted shut as usual, but there was also a ten-pound rock in front of the door. With one hand on the pistol butt again, Gonzalo kicked the rock aside and undid the lock. A small shock of air, hot and humid even in comparison with the hot and humid air of the day, hit him in the face, and he waved it away. He heard a small popping noise as the corrugated metal of the roof began to cool. He stepped into the darkness of the room and waited for his eyes to adjust. He estimated it was well over a hundred degrees, perhaps over 120, in the tiny shack. A trickle of sweat ran down his back. He found Samuel before his eyes had fully gotten used to the dark. In a corner opposite the door, the boy lay, cut, bruised, and motionless. Gonzalo rushed to kneel by his side, turned him over, and put his ear to the boy's chest. He looked up to the zinc ceiling.

"God damn it," he said slowly.

He rushed out of the shack carrying the boy and ran full speed to his car. He placed the boy gently on the backseat and got on his CB, trying to raise Collazo, hoping Hector would be in his car, but neither deputy was available.

"Come on," he yelled to Julio.

"Sit in the back with the boy. Make sure he doesn't fall off the seat."

The race to the clinic took only three or four minutes, but it seemed nearly eternal to Gonzalo. Finding the boy solved one problem, but his condition—possibly comatose like Lydia—brought its own complications. Who had done this to Samuel, who had killed and carried off Doña Perfecta, who had attacked Lydia, and whether any of these crimes were connected to each other or to the pedophiles currently invading his town, all of these remained questions that needed immediate answers. By the time he reached the clinic,

Gonzalo had decided he needed to call the sheriff of Naranjito for help. He simply hadn't figured out how to explain this to his wife.

Gonzalo pulled into the clinic parking lot, honking his car horn, and Dr. Perez and Irma Pagan, the clinic's head nurse, rushed out. They carried the little boy in, Gonzalo and Julio following close behind.

"The Villareal boy?" Dr. Perez asked.

"That's him," Gonzalo answered.

"What's the matter with him?"

"How am I supposed to know? You're the doctor."

"He's unconscious," the doctor said.

Gonzalo couldn't tell whether this was supposed to be an official diagnosis or the doctor was throwing it out as a possibility he wanted the sheriff to confirm or deny.

Dr. Perez put the boy on an examining table; the clinic in Angustias had only two beds, usually used for people recovering from minor ailments. The nurse went toward the supply cabinet; the doctor began a series of tests, checking reflexes and pupil dilation, pulse and breathing, pinching the boy's skin.

"Hook him up to a unit of saline," he told the nurse.

"What does that mean? What's wrong?" Gonzalo asked.

Dr. Perez continued his examination of the boy.

"Where was he?" he asked.

"In Doña Perfecta's coffee shack. Zinc roof, no ventilation, extremely hot."

"He's dehydrated, you know. That's his main problem. . . ."

"So a little water, and he'll be alright?"

"Not necessarily," the doctor said. "His dehydration is pretty severe. There may be complications. Aside from that, do you see this mark?"

The doctor pointed to a dark pinprick on the boy's left ankle.

"I think that's a scorpion sting; not deadly in itself, but I have no idea yet whether the heat-related trauma will be exacerbated by this bite. I can medicate him for it, and rehydrating him will not be a problem, but frankly, he needs to get to Ponce."

"Will the boy live?"

"If he ever gets to Ponce? Most likely. He's very young. Kids his age have rebounded from worse. Now, the important question is can you get him to Ponce?"

Gonzalo turned to leave the room.

"I leave trips to Ponce in your hands, doctor," he tossed over his shoulder.

Gonzalo went to a phone in the corridor, leaving the doctor with his patient.

Dr. Perez was silently happy. He wanted all three patients out of his care and into the hands of a larger facility with specialists and modern equipment. As soon as Gonzalo had made his phone calls and left, the doctor arranged for the removal of the children; the hospital in Ponce refused his request to take his most needy patient, the prisoner. The transfer of a prisoner required Gonzalo's signature on certain forms. Dr. Perez didn't push the matter; he was pretty sure Gonzalo didn't want to lose custody of his suspect anyway.

Gonzalo's first phone call was to his wife. She was with Mrs. Villareal, and he wanted Mari to bring Samuel's mother to the clinic before the boy was transported.

"¿Quién habla?" his wife asked.

"It's me. Is Isabel there?"

"Sure. You want to talk to her?" Mari asked.

The question made Isabel Villareal sit up in her chair, attentive.

"No, not really. Look, bring her to the clinic. We found her boy, but he's not too good. Just tell her he's here and alive. The doctor can fill her in. Hurry. The doctor wants to send the boy to a hospital in Ponce."

"Are you going to be there?"

"Nope. Now there's a murder to investigate. I'll tell you later; I need to get some help on this one. . . ."

"You going to get that sheriff from Naranjito?"

"I was thinking about it. Why?"

"I've heard you say she's smart, that's all. I know you're not going to call Molina, right?"

"Right. Now get moving."

Gonzalo's second call was to the sheriff of Naranjito. Her first words to him were harsh.

"I'm not letting that old guy go. He shot at an officer. I'm bringing him before a judge."

"I'm not calling about Don Alonzo. I just have some puzzles to figure out and frankly I think I need a little help."

"Oh. What's your status down there? Any word on the kids?"

"Sure. We have them both. They're in the clinic now. Both unconscious."

"So what's the problem?"

"I'll fill you in when you get here. We have a murderer out. At the very least, I could use another senior person on the scene for some patrolling and footwork, but, like I said, I could use some help thinking things out."

"I'll be over in a bit. The station house?"

"Sure."

Gonzalo tried calling the deputy mayor's house, but no one picked up there, so he drove to the station house, where Jorge Nuñez was pacing.

"Any word on the boy?"

"Samuelito is in the clinic, his mother's on the way. He's unconscious from dehydration, but—"

"Oh, thank God. I was beginning to think those animals had got him."

"¿*Los Macheteros?*"

"No. The other ones; at least *Los Macheteros* only kill children. Anyway, now I can get back into bed. This day started too early for me."

"Well, I'm sorry to say but it's going to be a little longer. . . ."

"Don't tell me another kid is missing. What are the chances of that?"

"No, no. Not another child. Doña Perfecta."

"Doña Perfecta's missing? She's eighty years old; she couldn't have gotten too far."

"No, no. She's not missing—"

"She's not?"

"Well, she is, but—"

There was the sound of a car screeching to a halt in front of the precinct, and both men stared at the door waiting for the driver to enter. It was Sheriff Ortiz.

"Mayor, sheriff. What can I do to help?"

"Sheriff, you made it here in ten minutes. That's impressive."

"You said there was a murderer loose—"

"Murderer?" Nuñez asked.

"Yes. I was getting to that. Part of Doña Perfecta's scalp is on the floor of her kitchen. There's a trail of blood from where she fell to some car tracks outside her house. It looks like someone put her body into the trunk of a car. That's why she's missing. We found the boy on her property, in the coffee shack. There has to be some connection between the boy and the murder, right?"

Gonzalo looked to the other two, but they were pondering the problem.

"I mean it couldn't just be a coincidence that Samuel was found on the land of a woman who was murdered, could it?"

Nuñez and Ortiz stayed in thought.

"I figure whoever put him in the shack probably killed Doña Perfecta."

"You know what I think?" Sheriff Ortiz said. "I think it doesn't matter who put the boy in the shack. He's still unconscious, right? Well, when he wakes up, he'll tell us how he got into the shack. That problem will be solved. I think you should concentrate on the murder. Find what evidence there is at the scene and treat it as a separate incident until Samuel can tell you different." Sheriff Ortiz folded her arms for emphasis.

Gonzalo looked down in thought a moment.

"Okay. You're right. I'm going back to Doña Perfecta's house to start a more formal investigation. Sheriff Ortiz, I need you to stay here for a while if that's alright. I need you to contact Sheriff Molina. He's interrogating the suspect David Poole. Molina can be a little difficult to get along with so I—"

"Molina? He's always been a pussycat with me. You just have to know how to handle him," Sheriff Ortiz said.

"Oh, okay. Even better. Anyway, if he gets anything useful, I need to know it. Also, Jorge, I'm expecting Hector back from San Juan. Try getting him on the CB. Another thing. Collazo is somewhere having lunch. When he's done, send him to Doña Perfecta's house. He knew her a little, so let him know what happened before he gets there, okay?"

"What do you want me to tell Hector if I get him?" Jorge asked.

"Just find out if he has anything important, that's all. Also, I think most people have already heard, but tell those who are looking for the children that they can go home now."

"Don't forget to thank them profusely," Sheriff Ortiz added.

Gonzalo drove off to Doña Perfecta's house, and the deputy mayor sat at the CB trying to raise Hector or Collazo but having no luck at finding either man. Sheriff Ortiz sat at Gonzalo's desk to make the call to the sheriff of Comerio.

Sheriff Molina was sitting on the chair at the side of his desk when the phone rang. He was out of breath and the hand he used to pick up the receiver dripped blood onto a paper beneath it. His face was flecked with blood and sweat.

"Yeah," he answered.

"Hi. This is Sheriff Ortiz from Naranjito. I'm calling for Sheriff Gonzalo. He's real busy right now, but he was wondering if you had any new information about the activities of the suspect you have in custody."

Molina, who did not have it in his power to refuse Sheriff Ortiz anything, told her what he knew about the hilltop shacks and the tire tracks. He told her that Poole had confessed to everything in reference to Roberto Roman, but that he really had nothing to do with the other children. He told her that a third conspirator had been helping him and Anthony Borden; one Julio Acevedo, Hispanic but not Puerto Rican. Poole had given a detailed description of the man; the man was a paid facilitator, not a pedophile. He was supposed to have secured a second hiding place to use for a day or two. Molina told her this and told her he knew the information to be true.

"How do you know? If you've been rough with the suspect, he might tell you anything you want to hear," Ortiz suggested.

Molina chuckled on the other end of the line.

"No, Sheriff. There is a point in pain when a man wants nothing more to do with lies. There is a point where pain becomes a purifying process. . . ."

"But—"

"Believe me, sheriff. When it comes to this, I know my subject."

Molina told her to go to the hilltop if she thought it would be useful for the case in Angustias. This is what she did.

While Sheriff Ortiz was on the phone with Sheriff Molina, Isabel Villareal and her husband arrived at the clinic in separate cars. Mari and Isabel had come across Tomas as he was slowly driving along the roads of Angustias, looking for his child. The two cars had sped along to the clinic, and Isabel and Tomas jumped out of their respective cars and ran for the clinic door. They went in to see their son together, cried together, got information from the doctor together, and together were relieved to hear that their son was expected to recover fully once he had rested.

When it was explained to them that the man thought to be responsible for their son's suffering was in a room at the clinic, they huddled together and decided it was not their concern. Instead of asking to see the villain, they asked to be left alone with their child so they could pray over him. Dr. Perez was happy to grant this request, though he had no faith in prayers for healing. He thought of miraculous cures as hogwash, but, in this case, far less dangerous, less nerveracking for him, than having the parents confront Mr. Borden.

CHAPTER EIGHTEEN

Before returning to Doña Perfecta's house, Gonzalo took Julio Chagara back home. He left him with a strict injunction not to leave the premises under any circumstances.

"What about the latrine?" Julio wisely asked.

"Okay, but only to the latrine and back, you understand?" Gonzalo asked.

Julio nodded his answer, and Gonzalo drove to the crime scene. There wasn't much in the way of evidence at Doña Perfecta's house for Gonzalo to find. There was a set of footprints: men's sneakers, size nine. There were some partial fingerprints in the kitchen, too large to be Doña Perfecta's, but Gonzalo didn't think they would be enough to identify anyone. There was no sign of the sneaker prints anywhere near the coffee shack. There were his own shoe prints, the prints of Samuel's sandals, and the small prints of a child's sneaker. Doña Perfecta's prints were not near the shack; the coffee in the sacks inside the wooden structure was old, picked perhaps two years earlier. The zinc roof and the bolt lock, however, were fairly new and clean.

Gonzalo sat on the ground a few steps from the coffee shack. He wanted to think out the problem before him. He reminded himself that his one great resource as a detective was his intelligence.

"There's nothing to this case," he told himself.

"Doña Perfecta was killed last night. Julio Chagara heard arguing here last night, the bloodstain fits the time frame. The body was taken away by car. The driver was the killer. He wore size nine sneakers. I can get a match for the brand of sneaker, I'm sure. Can I get a match for the tire brand? No problem. In fact, what do the tire tracks tell me?"

Gonzalo got up from the dirt and went to the tire tracks. He lay down on the ground next to them and used his forearm to measure out the distance between the tire tracks and between the front and rear impressions. He measured the width of the tire print with the span of his hand. He then compared these rough estimates with those of his wife's car. He was on his knees measuring out the length of his wife's Mitsubishi hatchback with his forearm when Sheriff Ortiz drove up behind him and honked.

"You okay?" she asked, getting out of her car.

"Yeah, I'm just trying to evaluate one of the few clues at the scene here. It seems that my killer was driving a car that was much larger than this one. I'm guessing American-made. From the length of it, I'd guess pre–oil embargo. What do you think?"

Sheriff Ortiz scratched her head.

"Don't you carry a tape measure?"

"Well, it's my wife's car."

"Right. Here." She produced a tape measure from her glove compartment.

"You should keep one for car accidents and such," she told Gonzalo.

"I have one, I said. It's just not on me right now," Gonzalo said, taking the tape.

Together they took precise measurements of the car's wheel base and length. They measured the width of the suspect's tires.

At the end of their measuring, Sheriff Ortiz stood up and tilted her head to one side.

"I could be wrong here—we can check to be sure—but I think these measurements fit a Chevy Malibu Classic, 1978. Big but not too old."

"How can you know that?"

"Remember last month, a tourist stopped in the middle of the panoramic road to take a picture? Caused a six-car pileup. I wound up taking measurements of all types of skidmarks. I could almost swear these numbers match the ones for a Malibu Classic involved in the accident."

"There could be several models with these numbers," Gonzalo suggested.

"Yeah. That's true, of course. I said we can check on it. My guess was just a starting point for further investigation, not the solution to all your problems here."

"Okay, but we can definitely rule out either of the Toyotas recovered today, right?"

"Oh, yeah. Doesn't necessarily mean we can rule out the drivers, though."

Gonzalo shrugged. The men he had in custody weren't going

anywhere. If they were guilty of this crime as well, it would merely lengthen the sentence they were already going to serve. The case was truly urgent only if the killer of Doña Perfecta was still at large.

"Want to see the crime scene?"

"Well, I'm supposed to go to Comerio to follow up on Molina's deputies' work there."

"A few minutes won't hurt anything."

They went. On the one hand, the scene of a murder is one of the most gruesome spectacles afforded by a profession filled with gruesome spectacles. It is a thing most would like to avoid. On the other hand, this is where the most clues were—what detective could pass up the opportunity to be the one who notices the crucial scrap of evidence?

Sheriff Ortiz took a quick turn through the house, looking into every room, touching nothing.

"The house is as neat as a pin," she noted.

"She was a meticulous old woman."

"Yes, but except for the kitchen, there's no sign anything happened here. No struggle, no forced entry. A bit strange, don't you think?"

"Not really. Think of it. First of all, this house is deep in the mountains. The road has only been here for a couple of years. She might not have been in the habit of locking her doors. Or, maybe the person who did this knocked, and she let them in. There wasn't much of a struggle because she was eighty and five feet tall. She was hit in the head with something sharp and heavy, probably an axe or a maul. . . ."

"Why not a knife?" Ortiz asked.

"Look at the scalp. There's a small bone fragment in there; a part of her skull came off with the blow. Not impossible for it to be a knife, maybe a machete, but I think a heavier tool is probable."

"Agreed. Hadn't noticed the bone chip."

"Well, that's about the only thing I've got to go on. A few foot-prints, a few partial prints, probably useless. I'm thinking of asking my Toyota suspects if they have any clues about this, but it's begin-ning to look like a long shot."

"Nah, I wouldn't say it's a long shot. Not yet, anyway. Mind if I take a look?"

She was pointing at the floor of the kitchen. Gonzalo shrugged. Sheriff Ortiz pulled her driving gloves from her back pocket and put them on. She stuffed her ponytail under her shirt collar, and got down on her hands and knees. Gonzalo turned away from the sight of her bottom in the air; it was a more pleasant view than he wanted to admit to himself.

"Ah-ha," she said, standing. "Can you tell me whose this is?"

She held a black hair, something more than a foot long.

"Probably Doña Perfecta's. It's the right length."

"Right length, yes; not the right width though. Look at it."

She held out the hair.

"Doña Perfecta's hair sample here is extremely fine. My hair is fine, but not that fine. But this hair is the coarsest hair. Thicker than yours. Do you know anyone in town, male, size nine sneakers, drives an old American car, hair this color, length, and texture?"

Gonzalo thought a moment. Angustias had more than nine thou-sand inhabitants, but half were disqualified by virtue of their sex. Half again were disqualified by their age. He could think of only a half-dozen or so men who had long enough hair, but none that drove large American cars.

"No one comes to mind."

"Then we're probably talking about an out-of-towner, right?"

"Okay, but I would have said that in the first place."

"Good, but now you should be pretty confident about it. Anyway, let me get to Comerio before Molina's deputies trample any clues."

Ortiz walked quickly out of Doña Perfecta's house and headed for her car.

"Oh, Gonzalo. Follow the tracks as far as they go. Maybe it'll do some good," she tossed over her shoulder.

Gonzalo thought about the advice. He had already checked the blacktop for signs of the car, with no results. He decided a closer look at the tracks could do no harm, so he toured the tracks on his hands and knees. He confirmed that the car did stop a long time at the side of Doña Perfecta's house. And that the car had turned around on her property. He traced the trail all the way to the blacktop. It was clear from angle of entry onto the dirt and grass that the car had come from the direction of the main road. This was no help, but then he noticed something that was of use.

At the edge of the asphalt, where the road and Doña Perfecta's property met, there was a rock the size of a man's fist that protruded from underneath the blacktop. The first time Gonzalo inspected the tire tracks, they all seemed to indicate that the car had gone out in the same direction it had come from. But there was a smudge of tire rubber not larger than his pinky nail on this rock, and the rock was a few inches from where the tracks should have passed. This was strange, and Gonzalo could think of only one interpretation. The car had made a wide turn upon leaving the property. The front wheels made tracks that appeared to go left, but the smudge could only have been made if the rear tires got onto the road slightly to the right.

To the right of Doña Perfecta's gate there was nothing. The road went on for a half mile or so, then became a dirt road, then a very bumpy dirt road. The blacktop had only been laid down past Doña Perfecta's house because there were people who lived beyond her, and they were building cement homes. Their attempts at permanency failed, however, and all that remained of their efforts were some concrete foundations, some stray cinder-block walls, and the road.

Gonzalo got into his car and slowly followed this road past Doña Perfecta's land. He wasn't sure what he was looking for. He didn't expect to find the car or Doña Perfecta. What he did find where the blacktop gave way to dirt was a recurrence of the tire tracks. The driver had stopped long enough to drink two Coronas and toss the bottles into a nearby bush; there was still beer in them. These Gonzalo carefully moved to his trunk. There would be time later for getting prints off them.

He followed the dirt road a quarter of a mile more until it became so bumpy he was hitting his head on the ceiling of the car every few yards. He got out and walked another quarter of a mile of it. It seemed to him unlikely that a car could survive this type of road, but then he knew the car he was tracking was a much heavier one than what he was used to driving.

This was a part of Angustias that Gonzalo rarely saw, and after walking a little while longer he wondered if he was even in Angustias anymore. In fact, from one clearing in the brush (the road had become very narrow), he was sure he could see a hilltop ahead with several wooden shacks. He was sure he could make out three squad cars and several officers milling about. He was looking at Comerio and the hideout of Anthony Borden and David Poole a mile or two away.

Gonzalo jogged back to his wife's car. He considered this a break in the case. Clearly, whoever had killed Doña Perfecta had taken her to the shacks in Comerio. This tied Borden and Poole to a second murder. It also gave a possible location for the old woman's body. And it showed where the killer had spent at least part of his time.

At the same time Gonzalo made his discovery, Sheriff Ortiz was noticing something at the far end of the hilltop complex.

"What's over there?" she asked one of Molina's deputies.

He took a long look and shrugged.

"Bushes."

"Yeah, but they're dying."

He took another look and shrugged again.

"They're dying bushes," he said.

Ortiz looked hard at the deputy and decided further questioning wasn't going to achieve greater clarity. She walked down a gentle slope and took a close look at the wilted bushes she had pointed out.

"These bushes are hiding something," she called out.

The deputies came to her side, and they worked at clearing away the dead branches and vines. As Gonzalo could have told her, there was a narrow dirt road between walls of thick underbrush and tall grass that led to Angustias and Doña Perfecta's land. Gonzalo could not, however, have prepared Sheriff Ortiz for what she found on this road.

"I'll take the lead," she said. "Two of you can follow me. The rest stay here. Now, you two report anything you think might be a clue to me, okay? I don't care how small it seems—a cigarette butt, a hair, anything. Understood? Good. Let's go."

For fifty yards there was only one clue. The same size-nine

sneaker had made occasional prints where rain had left puddles that dried into tiny bars of red clay dust. At a bend in the road, fifty yards in, there were a dozen empty beer bottles. There were also tire tracks matching those found on Doña Perfecta's land. These tracks led straight into the tall grass, running toward a *flamboyán* tree.

In the shade of the red-flowered *flamboyán*, the Malibu Classic sat, its driver asleep at the wheel. Sheriff Ortiz looked in the driver's side window. The driver, a Hispanic man with hair long enough and thick enough to match that found in Doña Perfecta's kitchen, had his head leaned back and his mouth wide open, and the sound of his snore was that of a man trying to clear his throat of a fishbone.

Ortiz took a step away from the car and cleared her throat, trying to get the driver's attention. He snored. She called to him.

"Sir. I need to talk to you."

He snored. Ortiz gave a glance at the deputies standing at the rear of the car and stepped to the driver's side again. She slapped the hood of the car. This time the driver responded by shoving his door open, knocking Ortiz over, and running a half circle through the tall grass around the *flamboyán* tree. The two deputies came to her side, but she waved them off.

"Get him! I'm fine," she yelled.

The grass was about six feet tall here, with leaves sharp enough to cut through skin and light clothing. It was difficult to chase anyone under these circumstances—once one lost sight of the quarry, it was almost impossible to pick it up again.

Ortiz jumped on the hood of the car before joining the chase. From there she could see the suspect was circling for the shacks and the two deputies were slightly off course and falling far behind. She jumped off the car and ran through the grass on a course to intercept the driver.

The driver made it to the clearing around the shacks two steps ahead of Ortiz. He was heading for the road off the hill. The other deputies—there were four of Molina's men standing around—did nothing. It seemed strange for someone to run out of the bush that way, but it didn't strike them as an offense that warranted action on their part; running through the countryside was not illegal.

"Stop him!" Susana Ortiz shouted, but it was too late. The man was fast and she was the only officer near him. She made a desperate attempt to tackle him. She lunged at him and pushed him from behind with a two-handed tag. It worked. He took four more steps and dove into the dirt headfirst. She scrambled to her feet at the same instant he did and just close enough that the punch he threw, a punch that started somewhere near the ground, caught her full in the jaw. She staggered back two or three steps and threw punches of her own, but they were wild, and he was already gone.

Sheriff Ortiz stumbled a few steps more but stopped. She pointed in the direction the driver had gone, and tried to yell instructions about following him, but her mouth wouldn't work properly. Molina's deputies crowded around her, asking if she was okay. She sat on the ground, frustrated.

The driver got away. The car had been reported stolen months earlier. The trunk was empty and clean.

CHAPTER NINETEEN

Hector Pareda had spent several years of his youth in New York City, but he hadn't spoken English on a regular basis since he was twelve. While Mrs. Borden raged in the back seat of the car, screaming about her rights and the mistake he was making, he didn't feel he needed to explain anything to her. It was his experience that there was little point in explaining things to prisoners in her state of whipped-up fury. He estimated she would understand him no better than a drunk would. It wasn't until he had gotten trapped in one of the legendary traffic jams near the San Juan area, *el tapón de Bayamón,* that she began to calm down, her anger spent, and he began to feel he needed to explain the arrest.

"Why are you doing this to me?" she begged for what seemed the hundredth time.

"You husman is a very bad man, and we thing you in a complot with him," Hector tried to explain.

"Anthony? What did he do?"

It should be pointed out that Mrs. Borden, only twenty years of age, had the idea that all Spanish-speaking countries had corrupt police systems. She had begged Anthony to take her someplace civilized. New York, maybe. She wasn't surprised that she, an innocent woman, had been arrested. She was simply terrified that she would be raped and murdered; worse yet, she envisioned being sold in some nebulous white-slave market.

"What did Anthony do?" she demanded.

"He kill a boy," Hector answered.

Mrs. Borden, Elaine, had been sitting forward in her seat, asking her questions directly into Hector's ear. This information made her sit back.

"What do you mean? He killed a boy? How?"

The question was difficult for Hector to answer. Had Borden used a gun or a knife, his crime would have been clear. As it was, Hector knew Borden's wife would interpret the facts of the case the wrong way. She would say it was all an accident. She would say that Hector was just as guilty in the boy's death as her husband; she would point out that they were partners in crime, that Hector deserved punishment as much as her husband did. And in his heart, Hector agreed.

"You husman kidnap a boy. A boy for sex. You understand? Sex?"

"What on earth are you talking about? Look, just tell me what Anthony is being charged with, okay?"

"No," Hector said. "You wait. The . . . Sheriff Gonzalo, he speak *inglés* better then me."

Mrs. Borden calmed down for a few minutes. Hector decided to cut past several lanes of traffic with Gonzalo's blue police light flashing. He drove along the shoulder of the road until he got to the problem that was holding up five thousand cars. A milk tanker had jackknifed and overturned. Three or four thousand gallons of milk had spilled onto the road. Hundreds of gallons were accumulated a foot deep in a dip in the road, and crews were trying to broom it all toward sewer drains. Hector plowed the car through the milk and around the truck, a maneuver Gonzalo would later say Hector would not have tried had he been in his own car.

When they had gotten around the pool of spilled milk, Elaine Borden moved up to the edge of her seat again.

"Can you tell me what I'm being charged with?" she asked.

"I thing you help you husman. A *complot*. You understand? *Complot*."

"What is that? I don't understand. I helped my husband do what?"

"Conspiracy," Hector said as clearly as he could.

"Conspiracy? To do what? To kill a boy? I swear, we did not kill anyone. Impossible. You understand? Impossible."

"Wait. The sheriff, he explain everything."

Mrs. Borden sat back quietly in her seat for a few minutes. When Hector started to drive into the hills toward Angustias, she began to cry. The deputy wanted to tell her everything was going to be alright. It was very easy for him to believe that she knew nothing of Anthony Borden's activities. While it was strange that Borden would bring his wife along on a trip where he was going to hunt down an innocent child for his gross sexual purposes, Elaine Borden seemed to have played no role in his plans. The young lady crying in his rearview mirror appeared almost as much a victim of Anthony Borden's depravity as Roberto Roman had been.

Once Hector drove into Angustias, he realized he had no idea where in Angustias to take his prisoner. It didn't seem appropriate to lock up an innocent woman in the precinct jail cell. It would have been impossible to take her directly to Gonzalo since he didn't know where the sheriff was. The prisoner herself offered a temporary solution.

"Can I see my husband, please?" she sniffled.

Hector headed for the clinic.

"Is Anthony hurt?" she asked as Hector parked.

"Yes," Hector answered.

He led her out of the car and took off her handcuffs. It didn't seem useful to keep them on her, but he made sure she saw the handgun at his side. For her part, she would have rather had the handcuffs on than be menaced with deadly force. She understood his message that she should try nothing suspicious while free of her restraints.

The clinic waiting area had several patients hoping to see the doctor. Though the regular appointments had all been canceled for the day, these were people who had walked in with various ailments that they thought needed immediate care. The waiting area's seats also held the Romans, still crying bitterly, and Mari and the Villareals. When Hector walked in with Mrs. Borden, all the waiters turned to them. With her mascara running and her nose red, Mrs. Borden looked to the Romans and the Villareals like a fellow sufferer.

The mechanic Luis Velez was at that moment trying to get the respirator to work again. After breaking down every ten minutes for an hour, the machine had become fairly reliable. It had sputtered to a halt just a half minute before Elaine Borden walked into her husband's room.

"What's he doing?" she asked Dr. Perez, pointing at Velez.

"He's fixing the respirator," Dr. Perez answered matter-of-factly.

"Anthony's on a respirator?"

"It's fixed," Velez said.

He wanted to add that the whole problem was a single gear that refused to stay properly aligned, but he reasoned, correctly, that if the doctor knew this he would fix it himself.

"Go out to the waiting area. Get yourself a coffee. We'll call you if we need you again," the doctor told Velez.

Velez complied. Even at an exorbitant rate of pay, he was beginning to tire of working the little gear back into place with his thumbnail. Once in a waiting-room chair, he promptly fell to snoring.

Elaine went to her husband's side and put a hand to his cheek. She looked into his face with a new bride's love. Now, when he most felt his wife's love and sympathy, he felt least deserving of her care. He understood at that moment how very far the concentric circles of pain emanated from his actions of that morning. He was fully aware that his wife's feelings for him would change the moment she learned all that he had done. He knew her heart would harden against him, her wellspring of kind emotions would dry, and he would finally be outcast from every corner of humanity. What else could he do but close his eyes and, as far as he was able, lean his face into the palm of her then loving hand, coveting all the affection and concern she shone upon him? And when the doctor touched her arm and she kissed Anthony's forehead, saying she would be back soon, what else could he do but wish himself already dead?

"What's wrong with him?" was Elaine's first question.

The doctor had called her out into the hall because he felt it his duty to explain Anthony Borden's condition, but he knew the explanation would lead him into a discussion of the abduction and car chase. He paused a moment, trying to think of a way to avoid this part while still being frank with his patient's wife.

"Your husband's neck is broken. There is swelling around some of the nerves that are located in his neck. Essentially, he is paralyzed, and, barring a miracle, the way you see him now is the way he will always be."

Elaine raised a trembling hand to her lips.

"Oh my God," was all she could say.

"The good news is that he can understand everything you say to him. His mind is not affected. If you talk to him, he can answer by blinking; you know, one for 'yes,' two for 'no.'" Dr. Perez demonstrated.

"How . . . how did this happen?" she asked next.

"I don't know all the details. I only know there was a car crash. Maybe you should talk to the deputy." Passing the buck seemed the most prudent course of action.

"The one waiting in Anthony's room? He won't tell me anything. He put me under arrest. He's not going to tell me what happened."

At that moment, Emilio Collazo walked into the clinic. He was looking for the Villareals to begin the search for the boyfriend his fellow diners had told him of. His appearance was a relief to the doctor, who was beginning to worry that he would be drawn into a discussion of a criminal case that he knew little about. He waved for Collazo to come to him.

"*Ésta es la esposa de Anthony Borden,*" he told Collazo. *This is the wife of Anthony Borden.* "Officer Pareda brought her over from San Juan. She wants to know how Borden got hurt."

Collazo shrugged.

"I don't know how to speak English," he said.

"I know that. I'll translate for you," the doctor said.

"You speak English?" Collazo asked.

"Sure. I went to medical school in Chicago. I'll translate, but I'm afraid of giving her inaccurate information."

"Where's the boy?" Collazo asked.

The doctor called Hector to the hallway.

"What do you know about this woman, son? Does she know anything?"

"I don't think she knows anything about her husband. I think she's innocent."

"Then let's tell her what happened."

There was nothing Hector wanted to do less than explain what had happened that afternoon. He couldn't think of a way of explaining the story that would make him seem blameless in the events that led to the death of Roberto Roman. In his mind, the story sounded something like, "Your husband abducted the boy, and I killed the boy."

"You tell her," Hector said, and he walked back into Anthony's room.

Collazo explained as much as was needed to make Elaine Borden aware of the enormity of her husband's actions. Still, she had some difficulty accepting that her husband could be involved in such a conspiracy. After all, he was on his honeymoon; they had had sex every night, every morning for that last week. He was satisfied if any man was ever satisfied, she explained. The doctor tried to make her think of pedophilia as an illness Anthony had. There was no connection to her, he told her. There were psychological issues involved that she could not have foreseen or forestalled. This was, of course, impossible to accept about someone she knew so well. They had the wrong man; he was only giving the boy a lift; some other explanation must be available.

Then they talked to her about David Poole. Their description fit a man she had once seen talking to Anthony in a restaurant: short, round, and red.

Even with the information that there was a picture of this man with a child, even with the information that Borden had this picture among his personal effects, Elaine Borden found it difficult to see her husband the way Collazo saw him.

"It can't be him. I don't know Poole; he was Anthony's friend. Maybe Poole gave him the envelope and Tony didn't know what was inside. Maybe . . . maybe he was just giving the boy a ride home. He said he was going to visit friends living in some town. Ponce, I think he said. He was going to be back . . . my God, he was going to be back now. This is a mistake; I know it is."

Mrs. Borden put her back to the wall and slid down into a sitting position. It took all her courage to believe what she was saying, and her nerves were clearly strained by the effort. She held her forehead and cried. This was too much for Collazo, who had endured a long day and knew there was much left to do before he could find any rest. He crouched beside her and yelled.

"Woman. Think of what you're saying. Do you think anyone believes such . . . such shit?"

Since he said all this in Spanish, Elaine could only guess at his meaning. Her guess was accurate, and she looked at him in dismay.

Collazo looked to the doctor.

"Interpret this. She says he went to visit a friend. Did he say who? Did he give an address? Did she know about his Puerto Rican friends before she got on the plane? Where does he know these people from? Why didn't she go with him if they're such good friends?"

The doctor interpreted all this faithfully, but Elaine shook her head and shrugged at each question. The people in the waiting room had moved to the head of the hallway to watch the spectacle; even Hector was looking on.

"No answer, little girl?" Collazo spat out.

"Come with me," he said, grabbing her by the wrist.

Collazo pulled her off the floor and dragged her to the end of the hallway to the doctor's office.

"Look," he said and pushed her to the ground near the sofa where Roberto Roman lay.

"Oh my God," she said.

She pushed herself away from the body, but Collazo caught her as she tried to slide across the floor. He dug his hands into her armpits and pulled her up to Roberto's face. He held her with one hand and pointed at the child with the other.

"Look!" he yelled. "Your husband did this! He killed this child! He killed this child, and if the boy hadn't died, he would be getting raped right now. He's better off. Even though his head is smashed and his body is broken, he was lucky. You understand me?"

Collazo's face was contorted with rage and streaked with hot tears.

"Interpret this," he told the doctor without looking up.

The doctor did interpret, but he didn't have to. Mrs. Borden had burst into tears with a glance at the boy's body. She understood everything now in the way Collazo understood it and needed no more convincing. She had awakened from a wedding cake and honeymoon dream to find her spouse was a monster worse than anything created by the mere imagination of man.

She looked around the room slowly, finding the face of Collazo and the doctor, of the nurse and the Romans. She could see in the eyes of Carmen Fernandez, the Villareals, and Mari that she was a pitiable thing. She saw torture in the face of the younger deputy, and Hector turned from her and left the room.

"Lie down, girl," Collazo said, and he eased her to a comfortable position on the floor.

"Give her something for her nerves, doctor. Tell her she'll be taken back to her hotel later. I'll have Officer Pareda take her to the station house to get an official statement, but I don't think we'll want her for much more soon. Maybe tomorrow. Tell her, okay?" Collazo said.

He walked out of the doctor's office to find Hector. He found the younger deputy in Anthony Borden's room. He was crying and making the small noise of a hurt puppy. Collazo spoke to him softly.

"What's the matter, son?"

"Nothing."

"That's not an answer, Pareda."

"I . . . nothing."

"Try again."

"Nothing. I just . . . I just killed the boy. I killed the boy, not Borden. Whatever Borden did to that boy, I helped him do it. You understand me? I looked at the boy's body just now; when the woman was looking at it. Did you see what I did? Did you see it? My God. I did that."

"Nonsense, son—"

"I did it. Borden didn't decide to go off the mountain. He didn't want to hit the tree. I did that. You understand me? The boy would be alive if I hadn't done what I did."

"So you think you're as bad as Borden?"

"Yes."

"That's ridiculous. What Borden did was done with the intention of taking advantage of the boy; what you did was done with the intention of helping. . . ."

"Yeah?"

"Yeah."

"Good," Hector said. "Then let's go ask the boy if my intentions mean anything to him. Oh! I'm sorry. I forgot. He's dead."

Collazo tried to touch his arm, but Hector pulled away and turned on him with a fierce look.

"Give it up, old man. Go away. One of us has to die. It's Borden or me because we're partners in death, and I can't stand it. I've been trying get the courage to kill Borden since I got in here, but I can't. Maybe it'll be me. . . ."

"Shut up, boy. You have work to do. I need you now. You want to die? Maybe tomorrow, but right now, someone has to get a statement from Mrs. Borden about what she knows. Someone has to take her back to San Juan. I've got things to do. You want to die? Do it later, when there's time. For now, go to the woman. Treat her nice. I don't think she even understands half of what her husband did. You understand me?"

The deputies had never spoken to each other with anger before. It was a new experience for the both of them, one they disliked. Hector paused a moment, but left the room as requested. Collazo had no authority to order the younger deputy to do anything, but Hector never failed to defer to Collazo's gray hair. Collazo looked up and sighed. He thought of praying, but the whirr of Borden's respirator stopped him.

He went to the prisoner's side, leaned over the edge of the bed, and looked into Anthony Borden's eyes. He tried to understand what he was looking at, but the young man before him was far too alien; he looked so calm, yet Collazo knew from sensational news stories that Anthony Borden was driven by animal urges and savage lusts. In something less than a minute, Collazo decided there was nothing in Borden's eyes that would reveal the meaning of the monster.

"*¿Quieres morir?*" he asked matter-of-factly. *Do you want to die?*

Borden had no idea what had been asked of him. Collazo scratched his head.

"Die, you?" he said in English.

He made the motion of turning off the ventilator. Borden understood and closed his eyes in gratefulness and nodded a centimeter in response.

The tube emanating from Anthony Borden's mouth was made of a clear hard plastic. This was attached to a flexible, ridged tube that stemmed from the ventilator. Collazo separated these two pieces so that the pumped air was a slight breeze across Borden's face.

Collazo stayed with him as the room began to darken, and the last thing Anthony Borden saw was the sign of the cross being made for him, and the last thing he heard was the soft word *"Descanse."*

CHAPTER TWENTY

The children, Lydia Fernandez and Samuel Villareal, were not going to Ponce. Two ambulances had been dispatched to Angustias, but they had gotten separated on their way and wound up in different towns in the hills of Puerto Rico, neither of them the right one. After calling the clinic to get directions, the drivers called again to say they were needed to attend to several firefighters hurt in a building collapse in Juncos. Lydia and Samuel, not being in an emergency condition, would have to wait.

After the first call from one of the ambulance drivers and while Collazo was in the bathroom washing his face again and again, Gonzalo came into the clinic with Sheriff Ortiz. He had an arm thrown about her shoulder and was hugging her tight to his side as he walked her in. Mari, sitting in the waiting area near the entrance, looked at him and raised an eyebrow about as far as it would go. The two sheriffs passed without noticing her or her eyebrow and headed for the doctor. Dr. Perez stood at the nurse's station. He was talking with Irma Pagan, the nurse, about his frustrations in getting the children taken away when Gonzalo interrupted him.

"Doctor. This is Sheriff Susana Ortiz from Naranjito. She needs a place to lie down a while, and I think she needs some stitches on the inside of her mouth."

Dr. Perez turned a weary eye to this next patient.

"What happened this time?" he asked. The day had been unusually busy for the tiny clinic.

"She was punched in the jaw. Very hard," Gonzalo said.

The doctor led Sheriff Ortiz to the second examining room. This was the very last available space in the clinic, and he thought to himself that if a single other person got sick in Angustias that day, he would have to treat them in the parking lot or the bathroom.

"Hop up on the examining table," he instructed.

"Good. Now . . . You can let her go now, sheriff; I need to examine her."

Gonzalo complied, but warned the doctor.

"She's a little dizzy still from the punch."

And she demonstrated by tilting back into a reclined position on the table. The doctor caught her by her shirtfront.

"Okay. Hold on to her. I want to take a look in her mouth. Okay, now. Open wide."

Sheriff Ortiz opened her mouth about half an inch, and a long string of blood and saliva poured over her lips.

"Okay. We'll assume you need stitches. Now. Can you open your mouth farther, or is there pain when you try?"

Ortiz looked at him with wild eyes. She tried to enunciate the word "pain" without opening her mouth again, and the doctor understood what she was trying to say.

"You say she was punched? Not hit with a baseball bat or something?"

"Nope. They told me it was a sucker punch; she walked straight into it. Is her jaw broken?"

"Well, had she been hit with something, I'd say yes. Since it was a punch, I'm going to guess probably no more than a hairline fracture given the placement of the bruise. If he had hit her an inch this way, or if her mouth had been open, she'd definitely have a broken jaw. We'd need to implant a brace. Very ugly. It gets screwed right into her face. Anyway, as it is . . ." He turned to Ortiz. "Let me see. . . . Open up again."

Another string of bloody drool dripped out of her mouth, but this time Dr. Perez grabbed her chin and pulled her mouth open and shoved it shut again. When she threw herself back in agony, he wasn't fast enough to keep her from falling flat on the examining table. Nor was he fast enough to keep from being kicked in the ribs.

"What did you do?" Gonzalo yelled.

The doctor straightened his body out.

"Her jaw was dislocated. Sorry, Sheriff. Believe me. It would have been much more painful if you had known it was coming. Excuse me."

Dr. Perez walked out to the hallway, where he stood doubled over a few seconds, then stood upright, drew several deep breaths, wiped away a tear, and prepared to reenter the examination room. Collazo came out of the bathroom, and the doctor waved him over.

"Gonzalo's inside. I'm going to the bathroom a minute."

Deputy Collazo opened the door to the examination room. He

had in mind already what he was going to say. As he went in, he saw the funeral director, Raul Santoni, enter the clinic and greet Mr. and Mrs. Roman.

"Your face is wet," Gonzalo said as the deputy came into the room.

"I killed Borden," Collazo responded.

Gonzalo was stunned and silent. Sheriff Ortiz sat up, still holding her jaw, looked at the two men, hopped off the examining table, and walked out of the room without comment.

"What do you mean, 'I killed Borden'?"

"I disconnected his . . . his breathing thing. The machine."

"When? Are you sure he's dead?"

"I watched him go. I said a prayer for him. He's dead."

Gonzalo looked to the ceiling as though hoping to find the next question there.

"Why?"

"Why?"

"Yeah, I said that. Why?"

"Because of the boy. Pareda was suffering. He blames himself for the crash. Because of you."

"Me?"

"You. I know you, Gonzalo. You're busy now, but you would have gotten around to blaming yourself. You would have gotten around to hurting over this crash."

"That's nonsense."

"You think so? Have you gotten around to seeing the body of the boy? You want to tell me you wouldn't have found something to make you suffer? Borden was alive, and you kept him that way. *A otro perro con ese hueso. No te creo.*" *Take that bone to another dog. I don't believe you.*

"Okay. Whatever. Look. Did you . . . Did Borden . . . Did he want to die?"

"I asked him. I think, in the end, he felt bad. I think he was grateful when I finally let him go."

Gonzalo paced the tiny room, thinking.

"Okay. Let me go see the body."

The two men walked to Anthony Borden's room. The doctor was there with Irma Pagan.

"Time of death, 3:13 P.M.," the doctor said to himself.

"It looks like somebody killed your prisoner, sheriff. Of course, I'll leave it to you to decide whether it was murder, but this plastic tube—"

"I've heard, doctor. It is my understanding that Mr. Borden wanted to be released. He wanted to die and let's just say someone helped to do what he wanted."

"Yes, but legally . . . ," the doctor began.

"Dr. Perez. You can appreciate that this was a special case. You know the patient wanted to die. He told you that much. You put him on the ventilator against his wishes, right?"

"But . . ."

"Then it might be best for everyone if we say he was removed from life support as per his request. It's the truth anyway."

Dr. Perez thought out his options and decided to agree.

"I can't imagine there'll be too many people who'll fight us on this," Gonzalo added. "His family's far away if he has any, and—"

"What about his wife?" the doctor asked.

"His wife? He was married?"

"Hector arrested his bride," Collazo said. "They were on their honeymoon. She didn't know anything, so I told him to take her statement and drive her back to San Juan."

"Oh. You sure about her innocence?"

"You beginning to doubt my judgment?"

Gonzalo ignored the question.

"So he was on his honeymoon, eh? When will the evil of this world come to an end?"

Collazo thought this last phrase especially appropriate, given his own sins of the day. There was still much to do, however, and he left the room with Gonzalo. Mari was waiting for them in the hallway.

"The boy's up," she said.

"Praise God," Gonzalo said. "That's the first piece of good news all day."

Samuel Villareal was more than up. He was angry. When Gonzalo entered the examining room he was in, the boy was gesticulating with more vigor than Gonzalo would have imagined for a child so small.

"She did it. She put me in there. I want you to do something to her, Papi. She needs to be punished."

The Villareals were overjoyed to see Samuel so emphatically alive. Isabel couldn't stop stroking his hair. Tomas had one of the boy's feet firmly in hand, and he was waggling it back and forth.

"Who did this to him?" Gonzalo whispered.

"Marisol," Tomas answered.

"Why?"

"Why? We don't know why yet. He hasn't explained that yet, but he's been talking steadily for the last few minutes. I'm sure you'll get a reason in a minute or two."

"I'll tell you why," the boy shouted. "I saw her with a boy. A few days ago. They were kissing. He put his hand in her shirt. I saw it. Marisol was talking to him on the phone, then she said I had to go to the *casita*. She was gonna get me out of the *casita* in the morning, before school—"

"Okay, but do you know the name of the boy she was with?" Gonzalo interrupted.

"Pedro. I don't know the rest of his name."

"Did he have his hair brushed back?" Gonzalo asked.

"Yes."

"Okay. Get better, little boy."

Gonzalo, Collazo, and Mari went into the hallway.

"Pedro Rios is Lydia Fernandez's old boyfriend. She lost him when he became interested in another girl. I'll bet anything the other girl was Marisol Villareal," Gonzalo said.

"And you think Marisol beat Lydia up last night?" Collazo asked.

"Either her or the boy. Still, there are some loose ends to tie up here. We need to hear from Pedro and Marisol. If they don't talk, we're still at square one in Lydia's case. . . ."

"Until she wakes up," Mari reminded him.

"Right. Well, I'm going to ask the Villareals if I can talk to the girl. Collazo, I want you to find Pedro Rios and ask him some hard questions. I want to know everything he has to say about his involvement with these two girls. I want to know where he was last night. Threaten him with arrest if you have to, and tell him we know he lied. When you're done, meet me at the station."

"He lied?"

"Well, I think he probably knew more about these cases than he told me. If he didn't lie, he certainly wasn't forthcoming with his information. Go get him."

Collazo went out to his car and drove off to the Rios home.

"Can I go home now?" Mari asked her husband.

"Not yet. I need someone to stay with Sheriff Ortiz. She got hurt trying to help us. I can't just abandon her here. When the doctor says she's ready to go, drive her home."

"Are you leaving my car?"

"Nope. 'Fraid you'll have to use Irma Pagan's car."

"She goes home in a little bit."

"It can't be helped," Gonzalo said.

He walked into the examining room again and spoke with Tomas Villareal. Both Villareal daughters had been taken to stay with Gonzalo's mother. Tomas gave Gonzalo full permission to talk to Marisol.

"Do whatever you want with her. Put her in jail if you want."

"Tomas . . ."

"No, I'm serious. I don't tolerate this kind of behavior from my children. She almost killed Samuel; she let some boy kiss her and put his hand in her shirt. What are you going to do with a girl like that?" Tomas asked.

"What are you going to do with a girl like that? You're going to love her. In the end, that's all parents can do. Look. You're upset right now. You'll calm down. Then you'll see how silly it is to ask me to arrest her. That said, I'll arrest her if I have to. You understand?"

"Yes."

"Good. I'm going now. You forget the anger you feel right now. Think of the blessing of getting your son back."

For Collazo, talking to Pedro Rios was a small ordeal. The boy feared the deputy. When he saw Collazo drive up in front of the house, he ran inside and literally hid behind his mother's skirt. Mrs. Rios was only too ready to defend her child. She was a divorcée at a time when there was little sympathy for women in her position and in a place where her predicament set her apart from the majority.

After a dozen years of marriage, her son was almost all she could call her own.

When Collazo knocked at the door, Mrs. Rios opened the door just enough to make her face visible as she said, "He hasn't done anything. He's not talking to you."

She tried closing the door against the deputy, but he had already put his fingers in the opening. He screamed in pain and pushed the door open in anger.

"I can get information from him here or in the station house. We know he lied to Gonzalo. That kid should spend at least a night in jail for that."

Collazo grabbed the child by the collar and began dragging him out of the house.

"No. No. Stop. I'll talk to you. I'll talk," the boy yelled, trying to pull away from the old man.

"Good. Now tell me where you were last night."

"In my room," the boy said.

"You're lying," Collazo said, and he slapped Pedro Rios across his left cheek so hard the boy teared instantly.

"Don't hurt my boy!" the mother said.

Collazo gave her a cold glare.

"Your *boy* is lying to a police officer. He can be sent to a juvenile detention center for that. A little slap is better. Besides, he needs it," Collazo said.

"Try again, boy."

"I went to Colmado Ruiz."

"Why?"

"I met Marisol Villareal there."

"Inside the store?"

"Behind it."

"When?"

"Eight-thirty. Nine, maybe."

"And what did you do?"

"Nothing."

Collazo grabbed him by his collar again.

"We kissed. We kissed."

"And Lydia Fernandez?"

"What about her?"

"What did you do to her?"

"Nothing, I swear. I used to be her boyfriend, but I didn't even see her last night."

Collazo slapped the boy again.

"I'm telling the truth!" Pedro said. "I used to be her boyfriend, but not anymore. Honest."

"What did you do after the kissing?"

"Nothing. I went home too. I didn't see her again until school this morning. I swear."

"What about her brother, Samuel?"

"What about him?" Pedro asked. He cringed, expecting to be hit again, but he really didn't know how to answer the deputy.

"Did you see him last night?"

"No, he . . . he saw us once, but not last night. He wasn't with her."

"You're sure?"

Pedro was sure. Collazo gave mother and son a stern warning about making themselves available for further interviews if needed. He warned them also that if the boy was found to be lying, he would certainly go to jail; then he drove off to find his sheriff.

Marisol Villareal was playing on the oversized front lawn of Doña Ayala's house when Gonzalo drove up. She stood and looked toward the sheriff as he walked her way. She knew why he was there, and she felt somewhat relieved to get this opportunity to discuss how things had gotten out of her control.

"I want to talk to you," Gonzalo said, pointing at her.

"I did it," she responded.

The sheriff wondered at the epidemic of confession he seemed to be encountering for the first time in his almost twenty years as a peace officer.

"Okay. What did you do?"

"Everything," she said.

"A little more detail."

"I put Samuel in the shack. He knew about my boy—"

"Pedro Rios."

"He told you?"

"Who? Samuel? No. I just guessed. Thank you for confirming it. Continue. What else did you do?"

"I had a fight with Lydia Fernandez."

"A fight? Why?"

"She said she was having sex with Pedro."

"Where was this?"

"The sex?"

"The fight."

"Near Colmado Ruiz."

"Okay. Wait a minute. What were you doing at Colmado Ruiz? When was this?"

"This was about ten. Maybe later."

"Wait a minute. Let me get this straight. First, you put Samuel in the coffee shack, then you were kissing with Pedro, right?"

"Yes."

"Where?"

"Behind Colmado Ruiz. Ruiz never checks his land; he never

goes up the hill. You could build a house on his property, and he would never find out."

"Okay, fine. When was this?"

"Eight. Maybe a little later."

"Then you finished with Pedro at what time?"

"He left around nine-thirty. A little bit before that."

"Okay. Did you happen to notice anything strange about Doña Perfecta's house?"

"She had a visitor. Someone with a big car. Nothing really strange, though."

"Okay. Then you fought with Lydia at Colmado Ruiz?"

"Yes."

"Why?"

"I saw Lydia outside."

"And?"

"And she said I stole her boyfriend. She said Pedro had given her a necklace like the one he had given me. She said she was having sex with him."

"Let me guess. A thin gold chain with a small cross on it."

"How did you know?"

"I went through her bedroom and yours. She's right, you know. She has the same chain. Anyway, continue."

"I chased her. She ran behind the store, up the hill. She ran to where me and Pedro go—"

"How many times have you gone?"

"Not many."

"Hasn't your mom told you about—"

"Yes! But I can't always listen to her. You know what I mean?"

"No. Continue."

"She knocked me down, see?"

Marisol lowered her knee-high socks to show two scraped knees.

"Then what?"

"Then I hit her."

"With a rock?"

"Right."

"Did you know she almost died?"

Marisol had nothing to say to this.

"Did you think of telling anyone of what you did?"

"Yes. But nobody asked me."

Gonzalo rolled his eyes.

"Have you learned anything from this experience?" he asked.

"Like what?" was Marisol's answer.

The question baffled Gonzalo. He laughed softly to himself. The thought flashed through his mind that all of mankind had been unable to learn anything from a thousand wars; if this child had learned something of value from a few minutes of violence, she would have been special indeed. He wondered if he had any lessons to teach her of his own.

He reached a hand out to caress her face, and he arranged a lock of her hair behind an ear.

"You have a very beautiful face, young lady," he said.

She smiled and blushed and looked away in embarrassment.

"You should try to have a beautiful soul," he said, and walked away to his car.

Gonzalo thought of what he should do with Marisol Villareal while on his way to the station house to meet with Collazo. He was certain a juvenile detention center in San Juan would do nothing to make her a better member of society. A full-fledged prosecution would do little but hurt her parents.

After deputy and sheriff compared notes, they agreed it would be best for all involved to delay any final judgment about what should be done with Marisol until Lydia Fernandez woke from her coma.

"But what will you do if her story confirms Marisol's?" Collazo asked.

"Recommend community service. Her parents will go for it, and she's in no position to argue."

"Doing what?"

"The library. Weren't you at the last community meeting?"

"I've never been to any community meeting."

"Well, the librarian asked for volunteers. I'll send her Marisol for a hundred hours to be worked out every day after school. She can shelve books and such."

"Make it two hundred," Collazo suggested. "One for each kid she harmed."

CHAPTER TWENTY-ONE

Sometime near midnight that day, perhaps even early in the morning of the next day, Sheriff Molina returned to his precinct. There was only one other person in the building; he had ordered the deputies of the night watch to report to the station at the end of their shifts instead of the beginning as was customary. The order was confusing to some but obeyed by all.

Daniel Poole had been seen by only two deputies since he was taken to the interrogation room. Late in the afternoon, the officers returned to the station house thinking they had stayed away long enough for whatever Molina had in mind. The sheriff walked out of the interrogation room apparently unaware that there were others present. He had stripped down to his undershirt, his body covered in perspiration and sprayed with blood. He saw the officers staring through the slowly closing door of the interrogation room.

"Get out!" he roared.

The officers scurried and left the station house without saying a word. That they would be silent about what they saw did not need saying.

The mass of Poole's body lay on its side on the floor, naked. Streaks of blood seemed to come from every part of him. As the deputies walked into the cool night air, they individually wondered what Molina was doing to the prisoner and why. They wondered what could have been so bad that it deserved the full attention of Molina's prodigiously painful skills.

Molina left the station house an hour or two later, only to return, out of uniform, clean, shaven, presumably fed, at or near midnight. He came with his pickup, a fifty-five-gallon drum, and a hand truck. He wheeled the drum quietly into the precinct.

He entered the interrogation room, where Poole lay still on the floor. He kicked the man awake.

"Would you like to get out of here?" he asked in Spanish.

"Yes," Poole whispered in reply.

"You have to escape. Do you understand? I can't just let you walk out the door, okay?"

Poole agreed. He was in no condition to walk out of anywhere, and he understood that it would be impossible for the sheriff to let a prisoner walk out in the shape he was in. It would cause all sorts of questions. Mr. Poole agreed to escape.

Molina next showed Poole the fifty-five-gallon drum. He laid it on its side in front of Poole, and the broken man dragged himself into the drum. Molina righted it, covered it, and spoke into it through a baseball-size hole in the top. His Spanish was clear and slow.

"I'm taking this can far from Comerio. I'm going to drop it off where it won't be found. Then I'm going to turn my back on this drum and never see it again, forever. Understood?"

"Yes," Poole whispered.

"Agreed?"

"Agreed," Poole answered.

Molina then tamped down the lid, using his fist as a mallet, and bent the lip of the lid to make sure it didn't pop open at an inconvenient time. He tilted the drum onto the hand truck and wheeled it out to his pickup.

The sheriff drove south to the coast to a dock near Ponce. A friend who never asked questions owned a boat there, and Molina had the keys to it. He wheeled the drum onto the boat and listened at the hole on top. There was the sound of restful breathing coming from inside. To Molina's apparent surprise, the same sound came from the can even when the boat's loud engines sputtered on. An hour or more later when Molina shut off the engines, Poole's small voice was heard for the last time.

"Are we there yet?" he asked.

"Yes," Molina answered. "I am."

The sheriff leaned the drum over so that it rested on the side of the small boat, then he squatted and grabbed beneath it, and with his bull's strength he heaved it over the side and into the ocean. There it rolled on its side, skidding atop the waves, taking in cupfuls of water through the hole on top.

It took an hour or more for the drum to fill enough to finally sink. Poole said nothing in this time, though he did make intermittent feeble attempts to push open the lid. He must have realized that there was nothing he could say, no remark of contrition, no threat, no begging that would not have merely amused Molina.

The drum sank like a rock once it had enough water in it. Molina opened a can of beer to salute the occasion, then started the engines again and headed home. He was in bed by four in the morning. He would have taken the next day off, but Gonzalo requested an informal debriefing. He went to the Angustias station house at eight in the morning and sat across the desk from Gonzalo.

"I'll need to talk to Poole to clear up a few—" Gonzalo began.

"Poole's gone."

"What? What do you mean 'gone'?"

"He escaped," Molina clarified. There was a shrug in his voice and in his shoulders. He had already written his report.

Gonzalo sat back in his chair.

"So you mean he won't be bothering us again?" he finally asked.

"Oh, I don't think he'll be bothering anybody," Molina replied.

"So it's safe to forget about him?"

"Well, he was never really charged with anything, was he?"

"Not by me. I haven't done any paperwork yet."

"Then it's safe to forget he ever showed his face in these parts. Believe me. He's not a threat to anyone."

Gonzalo thought a moment in silence. He had gone to sleep hoping to interview Poole again. He wanted to better understand this particular flavor of criminal thinking. His curiosity would have to remain unsatisfied.

"Anything else?" Molina asked. "I'd like to get back into bed."

"No. Not really. I just want to thank you and your men for the generous assistance given to the people of Angustias yesterday. I'm sure we're all in your debt."

"Believe me, Gonzalo. This case had its rewards, if you know what I mean," Molina said, and he bared his teeth in a smile.

Gonzalo imagined Poole's fate, thinking of him as being buried alive or lying naked on an anthill. In a blink, he saw Poole with a hatchet between his eyes. In the moment before he responded to Molina, he thought how horrible it would be to kill a prisoner in cold blood and still call oneself a police officer. He remembered what he had done to Borden in the car on the hillside. What an abuse of all that was right, to treat a human being in that way. How much worse, however, to gloat about it.

"I know exactly what you mean," he told Molina.

"Good. See? Sometimes we see things eye to eye," Molina said. "We're not so different that we can't work together when we want to."

He stood up and offered Gonzalo his hand. Gonzalo took it instinctively and regretted what he had done. He rubbed his palm for the rest of the day, and it was a long while before he could effectively rationalize the angry actions he had taken against Borden and the alliance he had made with the sheriff of Comerio.

The news of Borden's death took Hector Pareda by surprise. After returning Mrs. Borden to her hotel that night, he stayed away from Angustias. He bought a six-pack of beer and drove to the back of the empty parking lot of an oceanside shopping mall in the city of Arecibo. There he sat on the hood of Gonzalo's car, near the edge of a cliff, drinking and staring at the rough waves below crashing onto the rough rocks over and over. After his fourth beer in quick succession, he screamed at an incoming wave.

"You better bring me an answer!" he shouted.

Then he laughed himself off the car.

"I don't even have a question," he giggled out to himself.

He walked to a dune above the beach and threw the remaining beers onto a footpath used by fishermen.

"They'll think the tide brought them the best catch of the year," he said.

Then he threw up and collapsed onto the sand and slept until morning. It was ten o'clock when he reached Angustias, and, instead of going home or to the precinct, he kept to the edge of town.

He sat near a small pond, thinking of the chase and crash. He focused on the last press of the gas pedal, the kiss of his car against the rear fender of the Toyota. Had the car contained only Anthony Borden, only the guilty party, that maneuver would have been perfect. Hector sat near the pond for an hour, tossing in pebble after pebble, seeing the Toyota fishtail and go off the mountain, wondering what the boy's last thoughts were, wondering what the boy might have become. He blamed himself for the loss he imagined all humanity had suffered through his rashness, through his attention to a small voice inside his head that turned out to be wrong.

"It's over, son," Collazo said, walking up behind him.

Hector was startled.

"How'd you find me, old man?"

"I know every inch of these woods. You can't hide from me, not in Angustias."

"Yeah? You know this little hole in the ground?" Hector asked, thumbing toward the pond.

"Know it? I used to bring cows to this pond before your father was born. Come on, child. That pond has enough pebbles in it."

"I can't go into town right now. Not yet."

Collazo sat down next to him.

"Son, you think tossing rocks in the water's gonna do some good? You're wrong. I told you, you've done good already. Don't think of the boy who died; it's sad, but forget it. Think of the fact that Anthony Borden was a young man; he might have abused a hundred boys in his life, but you stopped that. That's a good thing. Think what that *sinvergüenza* would be doing to Roberto right now if he had gotten away. You saved that boy a life of suffering that I can't even imagine. . . ."

"I do think of all that. I understand what you're saying. But I'm gonna have to live with the death of Roberto. Why? Because I helped to kill him. Me and Borden are partners. Even if I put it out of my mind now, I'll have to go through it again at Borden's trial."

"There isn't going to be a trial."

"What are you talking about? Even if he pleads guilty, I still have to go to court a couple of times to—"

"He's not going to plead guilty either. Borden's dead. Stopped breathing last night."

Hector stared at the pond a full minute, his mouth open in disbelief. He turned to Collazo with tears welling in his eyes.

"Oh, thank God," he cried and leaned his face into Collazo's shoulder.

The older man put an arm around him. Hector's tears came in fitful sobs and gasps for breath that shook both men. It was only then that the stranglehold of guilt clutching at his heart began to weaken, and he began to believe that he had accomplished something worth the high price that had been paid. The news of Borden's death released Hector from an imagined complicity with the murderer. He felt then that he could enter the city with a clear conscience.

Hector's relief was the only circumstance that mitigated Collazo's feelings. He had spent the night tossing and turning, waking his wife beside him. Cristina wanted to ask what it was that kept him from finally resting. Emilio's problem clearly had some connection to the crimes investigated that day. What else could cause such worry? She wanted to help him resolve the issue and calm him, if not for his sake then for hers, but Collazo would never volunteer information pertaining to a case. Questioning him would only have made him cross and done nothing to end his restlessness, so she endured the night by staying as still as possible and hoping in vain that he would find it in his heart to take a blanket to the sofa. He fell asleep shortly before sunrise, but it was too late for her to get any use from what was left of the night.

When Collazo got out of bed early the next morning, his coffee and crackers were waiting for him on the table.

"Nena, ¿qué haces despierta?" he asked. *What are you doing up?*

She bit her tongue to refrain from laughing in her husband's face.

"Here's your breakfast. If you want bread, we have some in the refrigerator from yesterday," she said.

"Aren't you going to eat?" he asked.

"No, I ate already. I'll just sit and watch you."

He bit into a cracker.

"What are you going to watch me for? I know what I'm doing."

He raised his cup of coffee to his lips and missed. The coffee dribbled off his chin onto his uniform. He jumped up and tossed the cup back onto the table, spilling the rest of the coffee in anger.

"¡Caramba!" he yelled.

"Millo, Millo, *cálmate,*" she said, patting the coffee off his clothes with a dishtowel. "Calm down. This isn't like you," she told him.

He grabbed her wrist, not hard enough to hurt, but enough to make her look into his face with surprise.

"What do you know about what I am like?" he asked her.

His face carried an expression she couldn't identify. It seemed as though he were both sad and angry, ready to cry or kick.

"Emilio Collazo, I know you better than any person alive on this planet knows you. I know you better than your own mother knew you, may she rest in peace. If there's something I don't know about you yet, I'm willing to listen. If you don't want to talk to me, talk to

Gonzalo. If not him, then find a priest. God knows everything about you, even if I don't. Talk to Him."

Collazo's face relaxed as he seemed to consider the options his wife had presented.

"Okay?" she asked him after a minute. "Now let go of my wrist. I have things to do."

Cristina Collazo cleared away the things on the table and wiped it down, then went into the kitchen. When she came back, her husband was gone, and she was able to get back to bed and sleep.

There was a short line at the confessional, and no one was surprised to see Collazo at the end of it; he confessed weekly. When he got into the booth, however, and heard the priest call him "child," he could not continue. Across the partition there was the young priest, Hector's age or near it, who helped Arturo Perea with the duties of the parish. On other occasions, Collazo had had no trouble confessing to the young man. This instance felt different; he could not trust the voice of youth to guide him out of so desperate an abyss as he was in.

"Forgive me, Father."

"Yes, what is it, my child?"

"No. Nothing. I just can't speak to you. Is Perea at home?"

"Well, certainly, my child, but I am able to . . ."

Collazo had already left the booth.

On the street behind the church, Arturo Perea, the longtime priest of Angustias, had his home. It was a small, Spanish-style villa with a walled garden in the back. The house was not nearly as old as the church, but it had been old even when Collazo first saw it as a boy. In his old age, Father Perea had hired a maid, and she showed Collazo to the garden. Perea was sitting on a bench near the fountain. He was tossing crumbs of bread into the water.

"The fish are dead," Collazo noted.

Father Perea peered into the water where two fish lay at the bottom of the pool and two lay on the surface.

"You're right. Well, it wasn't a lack of feeding. Maybe they don't like bread."

"Could be," Collazo answered. "Don't really know anything about fish. I've only ever dealt with cows and goats and chickens. Pigs, too, but I hate those."

"Oh, you should learn about fish. They're so peaceful. So calm . . ."

"They're dead."

"True. Still, even when they're alive, they're very peaceful. I've had a few dozen in here the last few months. . . . But then you're not here to talk about fish."

"I'm here to confess."

"But isn't the young man, Father Moreno—"

"That's just it. What I have to say, I can't say to a boy."

"Oh." Father Perea looked down at the cobblestones visible between his feet.

"Help me off this bench."

"I can confess here if you want."

"No, I don't want. Take me to that bench near the wall. We'll use the climbing roses as a partition."

Collazo helped the priest to his position and went to the other side of the roses and knelt.

"Good. Now, what is it, my son? What troubles you so?"

"I've killed a man," Collazo said.

"Was it while you were doing your job?"

"Yes . . . No. It was *while* I was doing my job, but it was not part of my work. I didn't do it for self-defense. I didn't do it to keep others out of harm."

"Why did you do it?"

"I . . . I did it to help another human being . . . emotionally."

"Explain, my child."

And Collazo did explain what he had done and why.

"So you see, Father, I did it to stop the suffering of the boy and Gonzalo. Still, I know I was wrong. . . ."

"Yes, you were."

"But does it make any difference that the man wanted to die?"

"How can you ask such a thing? Was it his life to give and take or was it God's?"

"God's."

"Then . . . then it makes no difference who wanted what. While it wasn't technically murder—the ventilator is an extraordinary measure—to the Church, taking a person off of one is not a sin. Still, in your heart you wanted to murder. That is sin. It makes no difference what emotional and spiritual pain your friends were in. In fact, don't you yet know that pain . . . pain is sometimes the mysterious way that God chooses to work in a person's life. Sometimes pain really does shape and form a person; it can make them better than they were. I'm surprised that at your age you still haven't learned all these things."

"I've learned them now."

"Yes. I imagine you have. Why? You learned them because of the pain you are in. See? Next time your friends are in spiritual pain, send them to me; that's what I get paid for."

"But then what—"

"Shhh. Listen."

Collazo strained to hear, but there was no sound out of the ordinary.

"What am I listening for?"

"Shhh!" The priest raised a finger to his lips.

"See the hummingbird?" Perea asked.

"Yes. Of course, but—"

"Does it care about the past?"

"No, but—"

"Because God cares for it, right?"

"Certainly, but—"

"But you, too, are a child of God. Forget this man you killed. Worry and guilt will do nothing to bring him back. Even if he did come back, that would not change the fact that you once sinned. But forget him."

Collazo waited a moment, wondering if the confession were over. It seemed that Father Perea was intent on studying the flight of the hummingbird from flower to flower.

"Is that it?" Collazo asked.

"What? Oh, no. Certainly not. You know there is one more part to this confession."

"What is my penance?" Collazo asked.

"Do you know the 'Our Father'?"

"Of course."

"Then go home and say the 'Our Father.'"

"That's it! I take one life and my penance is an 'Our Father'?"

"I didn't say one," Father Perea reminded him.

"Then how many?"

"Say the 'Our Father' until you accept every responsibility it contains for you and believe in your heart every promise it holds. Say the 'Hail Mary' as well. Meditate on these things until you have taken them into your heart. You are old, but you still have much to learn from these few words if you say them well."

"Thank you, Father."

"Yes. Well, do as I have told you, but first take me back to my fish."

244

"They're still dead, Father."

"Yes, Collazo, I realize that, but they are also very peaceful."

Later that afternoon, when Gonzalo got home again after filling out a half-dozen reports on the incidents of the day before and taking a turn through the center of town, he found Mari in the bedroom. She stood before the bureau mirror in her bra and panties, and she was sucking in her gut and pushing out her chest. Gonzalo stood at the doorway and laughed.

"What are you laughing at?" she demanded.

"Nothing."

"Now I want you to be absolutely serious. Look at me. I want you to look at me and tell me exactly what Susana Ortiz has that I don't."

Gonzalo caught himself just in time to keep his first answer, "Youth," to himself.

"Nothing. She doesn't have anything over you. In fact, she's all bruised up and stitched now. I ask you, who would choose her over you?"

"Be serious. She has a better body than me. Everybody says she's beautiful, right?"

"Well, yes. A lot of people say she is beautiful. . . ."

"And she's smart?"

"Well, yes she is, but—"

"And she's funny?"

"Well, sometimes, but—"

"Do you like her?"

"Well, she is a nice person—"

"But do you watch her leave when she walks away?"

"Nope. Never. I look the other way."

"You're such a liar! I saw you bringing her into the clinic. You were all over her. But you know what she told me when I took her home yesterday?"

"What?"

"She said you were a lucky man to have a woman like me."

"Really? Why did she say that?"

"I don't know. Why don't you call her and find out? I'll tell you something, though."

"What?"

"I think she was right. You are lucky to have a woman like me. Shoot. Even with all that driving back and forth, all those phone calls, talking to all those people, I still did all the laundry, swept, mopped, and made dinner."

"I know. That Ortiz girl is pretty smart. She knows the lucky one in this marriage."

He put an arm around Mari's waist and pulled her close to himself.

"Let me go. I have things to do," she said.

He looked into her eyes steadily, seriously, until she stopped struggling against him.

"Mari. I will never let you go. Every day for more than twenty years, I have told myself that I am a lucky man to have known you. I lie awake some nights watching you sleep. I know my good fortune—no sheriff from another town had to come to tell me this."

"Good, because I made that part up. That Ortiz girl was so filled with drugs she never said a word to me. She just slept on the ride home, and you know what?"

"What?"

"She snores."

1-29-07